Huw   Lewis Prosser

THE MYSTERY
OF THE PANTOMIME CAT

HE TURNED TO GO—BUT BEFORE HE WENT HE TOOK A LOOK
IN AT THE WINDOW NEAR BY, AND WHAT A SHOCK FATTY GOT!

THE MYSTERY OF
THE PANTOMIME CAT

Being the Seventh Adventure of
the Five Find-Outers and Dog

BY

ENID BLYTON

ILLUSTRATED BY

J. ABBEY

METHUEN & CO. LTD. LONDON
36 Essex Street Strand W.C.2

First Published November 3rd 1949
Reprinted three times
Reprinted 1954

2.3
CATALOGUE NO. 5199/U

PRINTED IN GREAT BRITAIN

FOREWORD

THIS is the seventh book of the series about the Five Find-Outers and Dog. The others:

THE MYSTERY OF THE BURNT COTTAGE
THE MYSTERY OF THE DISAPPEARING CAT
THE MYSTERY OF THE SECRET ROOM
THE MYSTERY OF THE SPITEFUL LETTERS
THE MYSTERY OF THE MISSING NECKLACE
THE MYSTERY OF THE HIDDEN HOUSE
THE MYSTERY OF THE INVISIBLE THIEF
THE MYSTERY OF THE VANISHED PRINCE
THE MYSTERY OF HOLLY LANE

In all these books the Find-Outers solve different mysteries in their own way. Although the series is about the same characters each time, each book is complete in itself.

CONTENTS

I. AT THE RAILWAY STATION

LARRY and Daisy were waiting for Fatty to come and call for them with Buster and Scottie. They swung on the gate and kept looking down the road.

'Nice to be home for the hols. again,' said Daisy. 'I wish Fatty would buck up. We shan't be in time to meet Pip and Bets' train if he doesn't buck up. I'm longing to see them again. It seems ages since the Christmas hols.'

'There he is!' said Larry, and jumped off the gate. 'And there's Buster. Hallo, Fatty! We'll have to hurry or we won't be in time to meet Bets and Pip.'

'Plenty of time,' said Fatty, who never seemed in a hurry. 'I say, it'll be fun to be all together again, won't it—the Five Find-Outers, ready to tackle the next super-colossal mystery!'

'Woof,' said Buster, feeling a bit left out. Fatty corrected himself. 'The Five Find-Outers *and Dog*. Sorry, Buster.'

'Come on,' said Daisy. 'The train will be in. Fancy, we've had almost a week's holiday and haven't seen Bets and Pip. I bet they didn't like staying with their Aunt Sophie—she's frightfully strict and proper. They'll be full of pleases and thank-yous and good manners for a few days!'

'It'll wear off,' said Fatty. 'Any one seen old Clear-Orf these hols.?'

Clear-Orf was the name the children gave to Mr. Goon, the village policeman. He couldn't bear the five children, and he hated Buster, who loved to dance round the fat policeman's ankles in a most aggravating way. The children had solved a good many mysteries which Mr. Goon had tried to puzzle out himself, and he was very jealous of them.

'He'll say "Clear-orf!" as soon as ever he spots one of us anywhere,' said Larry, with a grin. 'It's sort of automatic with him. I say—I wonder if there'll be any more mysteries these hols. I feel I could just use my brains nicely on a good juicy mystery!'

The others laughed. 'Don't let Daddy hear you say that,' said Daisy. 'You had such a bad report that he'll wonder why you don't use your brains for Latin and Maths., instead of Mysteries!'

'I suppose he had "Could use his brains better," or "Does not make the best use of his brains," on his report,' said Fatty. 'I know the sort of thing.'

'You couldn't *ever* have had those remarks put on *your* report, Fatty,' said Daisy, who had a great admiration for Fatty's brains.

'Well,' said Fatty, modestly, 'I *usually* have "A brilliant term's work," or "Far surpasses the average for his form" or . . .'

Larry gave him a punch. 'Still the same modest but conceited old Fatty! It's marvellous how you manage to boast in such a modest tone of voice, Fatty. I . . .'

'Stop arguing; there's the train's whistle,' said Daisy, beginning to run. 'We simply *must* be on the platform to meet Pip and Bets. Oh, poor Buster —he's getting left behind on his short legs. Come on, Buster!'

The three children and Buster burst through

the door on to the platform. Buster gave a delighted bark, and sniffed at the bottom of a pair of stout dark-blue trousers, whose owner was standing by the book-stall.

There was an exasperated snort. 'Clear-orf!' said a familiar voice. 'Put that dog on a lead!'

'Oh—*hallo*, Mr. Goon!' chorused Fatty, Larry, and Daisy, as if Mr. Goon was their dearest friend.

'Fancy seeing *you*!' said Fatty. 'I hope you are quite well, Mr. Goon—not feeling depressed at this weather, or . . .'

Mr. Goon was getting ready to be very snappish when the train came in with a thunderous roar that made it impossible to talk.

'There's Pip!' yelled Larry, and waved so violently that he almost knocked off Mr. Goon's helmet. Buster retired under a platform seat and sat there looking very dignified. He didn't like trains. Mr. Goon stood not far off, looking for whoever it was he had come to meet.

Bets and Pip tumbled out of the train in excitement. Bets ran to Fatty and hugged him. 'Fatty! I hoped you'd come and meet us! Hallo, Larry, hallo Daisy!'

'Hallo, young Bets,' said Fatty. He was very fond of Bets. He smacked Pip on the back. 'Hallo, Pip! You've just come back in time to help in a super-colossal mystery!'

This was said in a very loud voice, which was meant to reach Mr. Goon's ears. But unfortunately he didn't hear. He was shaking hands with another policeman, a young, pink-faced, smiling fellow.

'Look!' said Larry. 'Another policeman! Are we going to have two in Peterswood now, then?'

'I don't know,' said Fatty, looking hard at
the second policeman. 'I rather like the look of
Goon's friend—he looks a jolly sort of chap.'

'I like the way his ears stick out,' said Bets.

'Idiot,' said Pip. 'Where's old Buster, Fatty?'

'Here, Buster—come out from under that seat,'
said Fatty. 'Shame on you for being such a
coward!'

Buster crawled out, trying to wag his tail whilst
it was still down, in a most apologetic way. But as
the train then began to draw out of the station again
with a terrific series of chuffs, Buster retired hurriedly
under the seat once more.

'Poor Buster! I'm sure if I was a dog I'd hide
under a seat too,' said Bets, comfortingly.

'It's not so long ago since you always stood
behind me when the train came in,' said Pip. 'And
I remember you trying to . . .'

'Come on,' said Fatty, seeing Bets beginning to
go red. 'Let's go. BUSTER! Come on out and
don't be an idiot. The train is now a mile away.'

Buster came out, saw *two* pairs of dark-blue legs
walking towards him, and ran at them joyfully.
Mr. Goon kicked out.

'That there dog!' he said, balefully. He
turned to his companion. 'You want to look out
for this here dog,' he told him, in a loud voice.
'He wants reporting. He's not under proper
control, see? You keep your eyes open for him,
Pippin, and don't you stand no nonsense.'

'Oh, Mr. Goon, don't say there's going to be
two of you chasing poor Buster,' began Fatty, always
ready for an argument with Mr. Goon.

'There's *not* going to be two of us,' said Mr.

Goon. 'I'm off on a holiday—about time too—and this here's my colleague, P.C. Pippin, who's coming to take over when I'm away. And I'm very glad we've seen you, because now I can point you all out to him, and tell him to Keep his Eye on You. *And* that dog too.' He turned to his companion, who was looking a little startled.

'See these five kids? They think themselves very clever—think they can solve all the mysteries in the district! The trouble they've put me to—you wouldn't believe it! Keep your Eye on them, Pippin—and if there's any mystery about, keep it to yourself. If you don't you'll have these kids poking their noses into what concerns the Law, and making themselves Regular Nuisances.'

'Thanks for the introduction, Mr. Goon,' said Fatty, with a grin. He smiled at the other policeman. 'Pleased to welcome you to Peterswood, Mr. Pippin. I hope you'll be happy here. And—er—if at any time we can help you, just let us know.'

'There you are! What did I tell you?' said Mr. Goon, going red in the face. 'Can't stop interfering! You clear-orf, all of you and take that pestiferous dog with you. And mind you, I shall warn P.C. Pippin of all your little tricks and you'll find he won't stand any nonsense. See?'

Mr. Goon stalked off with his friend Pippin, who looked round at the children rather apologetically as he went. Fatty gave him a large wink. Pippin winked back.

'I like him,' said Bets. 'He's got a nice face. And his ears . . .'

'Stick out. Yes, you told us that before,' said Pip. 'I say, Fatty, I bet old Goon is going to have a wonderful time telling P.C. Pippin all about us. He'll make us out to be a band of young gangsters or something.'

'I bet he will!' said Fatty. 'I'd just love to hear what he says about us. I guess our ears will burn.'

They did burn! Mr. Goon was really enjoying himself warning P.C. Pippin about the Five Find-Outers—and Dog!

'You keep a firm hand on them,' said Mr. Goon. 'And don't you stand any nonsense from that fat boy—regular toad he is.'

'I thought he looked quite a good sort,' said P.C. Pippin, surprised.

Mr. Goon did one of his best snorts. 'That's all part of his artfulness. The times that boy's played his tricks on me—messed me up properly—given me all kinds of false clues, and spoilt some of my best cases! He's a half-wit, that's what he is—always dressing himself up and acting the fool.'

'But isn't he the boy that Inspector Jenks has got such a high opinion of?' said P.C. Pippin, frowning in perplexity. 'I seem to remember him saying that . . .'

This was quite the wrong remark to make to Mr. Goon. He went purple in the face and glared at Pippin, who looked back at him in alarm.

'That boy Sucks Up to Inspector Jenks,' said Mr. Goon. 'See? He's a regular sucker-up, that boy is. Don't you believe a word that the Inspector says about him. And just you look out for mysterious red-headed boys dashing about all over the place, see?'

P.C. Pippin's eyes almost popped out of his

head. ' Er—red-headed boys ? ' he said, in an astonished voice. ' I don't understand.'

' Use your brains, Pippin,' said Mr. Goon in a lofty voice. ' That boy, Fatty—he's got no end of disguises, and one of his favourite ones is a red wig. The times I've seen red-headed boys ! And it's been Fatty dressed up just to trick me. You be careful, Pippin. He'll try the same trick on you, you mark my words. He's a Bad Lot. All of those children are pests—interfering pests. No respect for the Law at all.'

P.C. Pippin listened in surprise, but most respectfully. Mr. Goon was twice his age and must have had a lot of experience. P.C. Pippin was very new and very keen. He felt proud to take Mr. Goon's place whilst he was away on holiday.

' I don't expect anything difficult will turn up when I'm away,' said Mr. Goon, as they turned into the gate of his little front garden. ' But *if* something turns up, keep it to yourself, Pippin—don't let those kids get their noses into it, whatever you do—and just you send for me if they do, see ? And try and get that dog run in for something. It's a dangerous dog, and I'd like to get it out of the way. You see what you can do.'

P.C. Pippin felt rather dazed. He had liked the children and the dog. It was surprising to find that Mr. Goon had such different ideas. Still—he ought to know ! P.C. Pippin determined to Do His Very Best for Mr. Goon. His Very, Very Best !

II. A NICE LITTLE PLAN FOR PIPPIN

THE Find-Outers were very pleased to be together again. The Easter holidays were not so long as the summer ones, and almost a week had gone by before Pip and Bets had arrived home from their stay with their aunt, so there didn't seem to be much time left.

'Not quite three weeks,' groaned Larry. 'I do hope the weather's decent. We can go for some bike-rides and picnics then.'

'And there's a good little show on down at the Little Theatre,' said Daisy. 'It's a kind of skit on Dick Whittington—awfully funny. I've seen it already, but we might all go again.'

'Oh—is that little company still going?' said Fatty, with interest. 'I remember seeing some of its plays in the Christmas hols. Some of the acting was pretty poor. I wondered if they'd like to try *me* out in a few parts. You know, last term at school . . ."

'Fatty! *Don't* tell us you took the leading part in the School play *again*,' begged Larry. 'Doesn't any one else *ever* take the leading part at your school but you?'

'Fatty's very, very good at acting—aren't you, Fatty?' said Bets, loyally. 'Look how he can disguise himself and take even *us* in! Fatty, are you going to disguise yourself these hols.? Do! Do you remember when you dressed up as that old balloon-woman, and sold balloons?'

'And old Clear-Orf came along and wanted to

8

see your licence,' chuckled Daisy. ' But you had so many petticoats on that you pretended you couldn't find it.'

' And Bets spotted it was you because she suddenly saw you had clean finger-nails and filthy, dirty hands,' said Larry, remembering. ' And that made her suspicious. I always thought that was smart of Bets.'

' You're making me feel I must disguise myself at once ! ' said Fatty, with a grin. ' What about playing a little joke on P.C. Pippin ? What a lovely name ! '

' Yes—and it suits him,' said Bets. ' He's got a sort of apple-cheeked face—a nice round ripe pippin.'

Every one roared. ' You tell him that,' said Pip. ' Go up to him and say " Dear nice round ripe pippin." He'll be *so* surprised.'

' Don't be silly,' said Bets. ' As if I would ! I quite liked him.'

' I wish something would turn up whilst Goon is away,' said Fatty. ' Wouldn't he be wild to miss a mystery ! And I bet we could help Pippin beautifully. He'd *like* our help, I expect. He doesn't look awfully clever—actually he might not be so good at snooping about as Goon, because Goon's had a lot of experience, and he's older—Pippin looks rather young. I bet we could tackle a mystery better than he could. We've solved a lot now. Six, in fact ! '

' We can't possibly expect a mystery *every* hols.' said Larry.

' Let's make up one for P.C. Pippin,' said Bets, suddenly. ' Just a teeny-weeny one ! With clues and things. He'd get awfully excited about it.'

2

The others stared at her. Fatty gave a sudden grin. ' I say ! That's rather an idea of Bets, isn't it ? Larry's right when he says we can't possibly expect a mystery every hols. and somehow I don't feel one will turn up in the next three weeks. So we'll concoct one—for that nice round ripe Pippin to solve ! '

Every one began to feel excited. It was something to plan and look forward to.

' I bet he'll make a whole lot of notes, and be proud to show them to Goon,' said Larry. ' And I bet Goon will smell a rat and know it's us. What a swizz for them ! '

' Now this is really very interesting,' said Fatty, pleased. ' It will be a nice little job for Pippin to use his brains on, it'll be some fun for us, and it will be *most* annoying for Goon when he comes back—because I bet he's warned Pippin about us. And all he'll find is that Pippin has wasted his time on a Pretend mystery ! '

' What mystery shall we make up ? ' said Bets, pleased that her idea was so popular with the others. ' Let's think of a really good one—that Fatty can use disguises for. I love it when Fatty disguises himself.'

' Let's all think hard,' said Fatty. ' We want to Rouse Suspicions, first of all—do something that will make P.C. Pippin think there's something up, you know—so that he will nose about—and find a few little Clues . . .'

' That we put ready for him,' said Bets, with a squeal of laughter. ' Oh *yes* ! Oh, I *know* I shan't think of anything. Hurry up, every one, and think hard.'

There was silence for a few minutes. As Bets said, she could think of no idea at all.

'Well—any one thought of anything?' asked Fatty. 'Daisy?'

'I *have* thought of something—but it's a bit feeble' said Daisy. 'What about sending Pippin a mysterious letter through the post?'

'No good,' said Fatty. 'He'd suspect us at once. Larry, have *you* thought of anything?'

'Well, what about mysterious noises in Pippin's back-garden at night?' said Larry. 'Very feeble, I know.'

'It is a bit,' said Fatty. 'Doesn't lead to anything. We want to do something that will really get Pippin worked up, make him think he's on to something big.'

'I can only think of something feeble too,' said Pip. 'You know—hiding in a garden at night till Pippin comes by—and then letting him hear us whisper—and then rushing off in the dark so that he suspects we've been up to mischief.'

'Now, there's something in *that*,' said Fatty, thinking over it. 'That really could lead on to something else. Let's see now. I'll work it out.'

Every one was respectfully silent. They looked at Fatty as he pursed up his mouth and frowned. The Great Brains were working!

'I think I've got it,' said Fatty, at last. 'We'll do this—I'll disguise myself as a ruffian of some kind—and I'll lend Larry a disguise too. We'll find out what Pippin's beat is at night—where he goes and what time—and Larry and I will hide in the garden of some empty house till he comes by.'

He paused to think, and then nodded his head.

' Yes—and as soon as we hear Pippin coming we'll begin to whisper loudly so that he'll hear us and challenge us. Then we'll make a run for it as if we were scared of him and didn't want to be seen.'

' But where does all this lead to ? ' said Larry.

' You wait a bit and see,' said Fatty, enjoying himself. ' Now, we'll escape all right—and what will Pippin do ? He'll go into the garden, of course, and shine his torch round—and he'll find a torn-up note ! '

' Oooh, yes,' said Bets, thrilled. ' What's in the note ? '

' The note will contain the name of some place for a further meeting,' said Fatty. ' We'll think of somewhere good. And when our nice round ripe Pippin arrives at the next meeting-place he'll find some lovely Clues ! '

' Which we'll have put there ! ' said Pip, grinning. ' Oh yes, Fatty—that's fine. We'll lead Pippin properly up the garden path.'

' The clues will lead somewhere else,' said Fatty, beaming. ' In fact it will be a nice wild-goose-chase for Pippin. He'll love it. And won't Goon's face be a picture when he hears about it all —he'll know it's us all right.'

' When can we do it ? Oh, Fatty, let's begin it soon,' begged Bets. ' Can't you and Larry begin to-night ? '

' No. We have to find out what Pippin's beat is first,' said Fatty. ' And we've got to spot an empty house on his beat. We'd better stalk him to-night, Larry, and find out where he goes. Goon always used to set off about half-past seven. Can you manage to come to my house by that time ? '

' Yes, I think so,' said Larry. ' We have supper at seven. I can gobble it down and be with you all right.'

So it was decided that Larry and Fatty should stalk P.C. Pippin that night and see exactly what his beat was, so that the next night they could prepare their little surprise for him. Bets was thrilled. She loved an adventure like this—it hadn't got the frightened excitement of a real mystery, it was under their control, and nothing horrid could come out of it except perhaps a scolding from Goon.

Larry was down at Fatty's house at twenty-five past seven that night. It was almost dark. They were not disguised, as there was no time to dress Larry up. The two boys slipped out of Fatty's house and made their way to the street in which Mr. Goon's house was. P.C. Pippin had it now, of course.

The boys could hear the telephone trilling in Pippin's front room, and they could hear him answering it. Then the receiver was put down, and the light in the room went out.

' He's coming ! ' whispered Fatty. ' Squash up more into the bushes, Larry.'

P.C. Pippin walked down to his front gate. He had rubbers on the soles of his boots and he did not make much noise. The boys could just see him as he turned up the street, away from them.

' Come on,' whispered Fatty. ' He's beginning his beat. We'll see exactly where he goes.'

They followed cautiously behind P.C. Pippin. The policeman went down the High Street, and was very conscientious indeed about trying doors and looking to see if the windows of the shops were fastened. The boys got rather bored with so much fumbling and examining. Each time P.C. Pippin stopped they had to stop too and hide somewhere.

After about an hour, P.C. Pippin moved off again, having decided that no burglar could possibly enter any shop in the High Street that night, any-way. He shut off his torch and turned into a side-street. The boys padded after him.

Pippin went down the street softly, and then went to examine a lock-up garage there. 'Why doesn't he get on with his beat?' groaned Larry, softly. 'All this stopping and staring!'

Pippin went on again. He appeared to have quite a systematic method—going up one side of the road and down the other, and then into the next road and so on. If he did this every night, it would be easy to lie in wait for him somewhere!

'It's nine o'clock,' said Fatty, in a low voice, as he heard the church clock strike loudly. 'And we're in Willow Road. There's an empty house over the other side, Larry. We could hide in the garden there to-morrow night, just before nine. Then we could startle Pippin when he gets along there. Look—he's shining his torch on the gate now. Yes, that's what we'll do—hide in the garden there.'

'Good,' said Larry, with relief. 'I'm just about tired of dodging round like this, and the wind's jolly cold too. Come on—let's go home. Meet to-morrow morning at Pip's to tell the others what we've decided, and make our plans.'

'Right,' said Fatty, who was also very glad that the shadowing of P.C. Pippin was at an end. 'See you to-morrow. Ssssst! Here comes Pippin again.'

They squeezed themselves into the hedge and were relieved when the policeman's footsteps passed them. 'Gosh—I nearly sneezed then,' whispered Larry. 'Come on—I'm frozen.'

They went quietly home, Larry to tell Daisy, his sister, that they had found a good place to hide the next night, and Fatty to plan their disguises. He pulled out some old clothes and looked at them. Aha, P.C. Pippin, he thought, there's a nice little surprise being planned for you !

III. TWO RUFFIANS—AND P.C. PIPPIN

THE five children discussed their plan with great interest the next day. Buster sat near them, ears cocked up, listening.

'Sorry, old thing, but I'm afraid you're not in this,' said Fatty, patting the little Scottie. 'You'll have to be tied up at home. Can't have you careering after me, yapping at Pippin, when he comes by our hiding-place.'

'Woof,' said Buster, mournfully, and lay down as if he had no further interest in the subject.

'Poor Buster,' said Bets, rubbing the sole of her shoe along his back. 'You hate to be left out, don't you? But this isn't a *real* mystery, Buster. It's only a pretend one.'

The children decided that Larry and Fatty had better get into their disguises at Larry's house, as it was near to the garden where they were to hide. Then they could sprint back to Larry's without much bother.

'I'll bring the clothes along in a suitcase after tea,' said Fatty. 'Any chance of hiding the case anywhere in your garden, Larry? In a shed or something. Grown-ups are always so suspicious of things like that. If I arrive at your house complete with suitcase your mother's quite likely to want to know what's in it.'

'Yes. Well, there's the little shed halfway down the garden,' said Larry. 'The one the gardener uses. I'll join you there whatever time you say

—and we might as well change into our disguises there, Fatty. We'd be safe there. What are we going to wear ? '

' Oh, *can* we come and see you getting into your disguises ? ' said Bets, who didn't want to miss anything if she could help it. ' Do let's. Pip and I could slip out when we are supposed to be reading after supper.'

' Mother is going to the Little Theatre to see the show there to-night,' said Pip, remembering. ' We'll be quite safe to come and see you disguising yourselves.'

So, at eight o'clock that night, Fatty, Larry, Daisy, Pip, and Bets were all shut up in the little shed together. Fatty pinned a sack tightly across the tiny window so that no light would show. Then he and Larry began to disguise themselves.

' We'd better make ourselves pretty awful-looking,' said Fatty. ' I bet Pippin will shine that torch of his on to us, and we'll let him get a good look at our ruffianly faces. Here, Larry—you wear this frightful moustache. And look, there's that red wig of mine—wear that too, under an old cap. You'll look horrible.'

Bets watched the two boys, fascinated. Fatty was extremely clever at dressing up. He had many books on the art of disguising oneself, and there wasn't much he didn't know about it ! Also he had a wonderful collection of false eyebrows, moustaches, beards, and even sets of celluloid teeth that fitted over his own teeth, and stuck out horribly.

He put on a ragged beard. He screwed up his face and applied black grease-paint to his wrinkles.

He stuck on a pair of shaggy eyebrows, which immediately altered him beyond recognition. Bets gave a squeal.

'You're horrible, Fatty! I don't know you. I can't bear to look at you.'

'Well, don't then,' said Fatty, with a grin that showed black gaps in his front teeth. Bets stared in horror.

'Fatty! Where are your teeth? You've got two missing!'

'Just blacked them out, that's all,' said Fatty, with another dreadful grin. 'In this light it looks as if I've got some missing, doesn't it?'

He put on a wig of thinnish hair that straggled under his cap. He screwed up his face, and waggled his beard at Bets and Daisy.

'You look disgusting and very frightening,' said Daisy. 'I'm glad I'm not going to walk into you unexpectedly to-night. I'd be scared stiff. Oh, look at Larry, Bets—he's almost as bad as Fatty. Larry, *don't* squint like that.'

Larry was squinting realistically, and had screwed up his mouth so that his moustache was all on one side.

'Don't overdo it,' said Fatty. 'You look like an idiot now—not that that's much change for you.'

Larry hit him on the back. 'You mind what you say to me,' he growled, in a deep voice. 'I'm Loopy Leonard from Lincoln.'

'You look it,' said Daisy. 'You're both horrible. Pippin won't believe you're real when he sees you!'

Fatty looked at Daisy. 'Do you think he'll

BETS WATCHED THE TWO BOYS, FASCINATED. FATTY WAS
EXTREMELY CLEVER AT DRESSING UP

see through our disguises then ? ' he asked, anxiously.
' Have we overdone it ? '

' No. Not really,' said Daisy. ' I mean, a
policeman sees lots of awful ruffians and scoundrels,
I expect, and some of them must look as bad as
you. Ugh, you do look revolting. I shall dream
about you to-night.'

' I say—time's getting on,' said Pip, suddenly,
looking at his watch. He had been silent and a
little sulky because he was not going too. But,
as Fatty pointed out, he was not tall enough to pass
for a man, whereas he and Larry were. They
were both well grown, and Fatty especially was
quite burly now.

' Right. We'll go,' said Fatty, and Larry opened
the door of the shed cautiously.

' We'll have to go past the kitchen door,' he
said. ' But it's all right, no one will hear us.'

The two horrible-looking ruffians tiptoed up
the path and round by the kitchen door. Just
as they got there the door opened and a bright
beam of light fell on the two of them. There was a
loud scream and the door was banged shut.

' Golly ! That was Janet, our cook,' whispered
Daisy. ' She must have had the fright of her life
when she saw you. Quick, get off before she tells
Daddy ! '

The two boys scurried away into the road.
Bets went home with Pip. Daisy went in at the
garden door and heard Janet telling her father
in a most excited voice about the two frightful men
she had seen. ' Great big fellows, sir,' she said,
' about six feet high, they were—and they glared
at me out of piercing eyes, and growled like dogs.'

Daisy chuckled and slipped upstairs. She wasn't at all surprised at Janet's horror. Those two certainly had looked dreadful.

Fatty and Larry made their way cautiously to the empty house. They crossed over whenever they heard any one coming along the dark streets. Nobody saw them, which was a good thing, for most people would certainly have raised the alarm at the sight of two such extraordinary-looking rogues.

They came to the empty house. They slipped in at the front gate very quietly indeed. There was a side gate as well.

' When Pippin comes by, we'll start our whispering here, under this bush,' said Fatty. ' And then when he comes in at the front gate to investigate, we'll sprint out of the side gate. Let him shine his light on our faces, because he can't possibly tell who we are, in these frightful disguises.'

' Right,' said Larry. ' Got the torn-up note, Fatty ? '

Fatty felt in his pocket. He drew out an envelope. In it was a dirty piece of paper, torn into six or eight pieces. On it Fatty had written a cryptic message.

' Behind Little Theatre. Ten p.m. Friday.'

He grinned as he took out the torn pieces and thought of the message on them. ' When Pippin turns up behind the Little Theatre on Friday we'll see that he finds a lovely lot of clues,' he said to Larry. He scattered the bits of paper on the ground below the bush they were hiding behind. They fell there and lay waiting for the unsuspicious Pippin to pick them up later on in the evening !

' Sh ! ! ' said Larry, suddenly. ' He's coming. I know his funny little cough now, though I can't hear his footsteps. Ah—now I can.'

The boys waited silently until P.C. Pippin was near the garden. Then Fatty said something in a sibilant whisper. Larry then rustled the bush. Fatty said ' Ssssst ! ' and P.C. Pippin switched on his torch at once.

' Now then ! Who's there ? You come on out and show yourselves ! ' said Pippin's voice, sounding very sharp indeed.

' Don't run yet,' whispered Fatty. ' Let him get a look at us.'

Larry rustled the bush again. Pippin turned his torch on to it at once, and was horrified to see two such villainous faces peering out at him. What ruffians ! Up to no good, *he'd* be bound !

' Now for it ! ' said Fatty, as the policeman swung open the front gate.

The two boys at once sprinted out of the back gate, and raced off down the road, with P.C. Pippin a very bad third. ' Hey, stop there ! Stop ! ' he shouted. This was more than the boys had bargained for ! Suppose somebody *did* stop them ! It would be very awkward indeed.

But fortunately no one stopped them or even tried to, though the village butcher, out for a walk with his wife in the fine spring night, did step out to catch hold of them. But when he saw Fatty's horrible-looking face in the light of a street-lamp he thought better of it, and the boys raced by in safety.

They turned in at Larry's gate thankfully. They went to the little shed and sank down, panting. Fatty grinned.

' Nice work, Larry ! He'll go back there with his torch and snoop round—and he'll find the torn bits of paper and turn up on time for his next clues on Friday. I enjoyed that. Did you ? '

' Yes,' said Larry. ' I only wish I didn't have to take off this wizard disguise. Can't we go round the town a bit and show ourselves to a few more people ? '

' Better not,' said Fatty. ' Come on—let's take our things off. My word—I wish it had been old Goon who came along and spotted us—what a thrill for him ! '

Meanwhile P.C. Pippin had made his way back to the garden where the two ruffians had been hiding. He was excited. He had never hoped for anything to happen whilst he was taking Goon's place. And now he had surprised two horrible-looking villains hiding in the garden of an empty house, no doubt planning a burglary of some kind.

P.C. Pippin shone his torch on the ground under the bush where the two ruffians had stood. He hoped to see some footprints there. Aha, yes —there were plenty ! And there was something else too—torn pieces of paper ! Could those fellows have dropped them ?

Mr. Pippin took his note-book from his pocket and placed the bits of paper carefully in the flap at the back. There were eight pieces—with writing on them ! He would examine them carefully at home. Next he took out a folding ruler and carefully measured the footprints in the soft earth. Then he looked about for cigarette-ends or any other clue. But except for the bits of paper there was nothing.

P.C. Pippin was up till past midnight piecing together the bits of paper, making out the thrilling message, writing out a description of the two men, and trying to draw the footprints to measure. He felt very important and pleased. This was his first Case. He was going to handle it well. He would go to that Little Theatre on Friday night, long before ten—and see what he would find there! All this might be Very, Very Important.

IV. PLENTY OF RED-HEADS—AND
PLENTY OF CLUES!

THE five children chuckled over the trick they had played on the unsuspecting Pippin. Larry had met him the morning after, and stopped to have a few words with him.

Mr. Pippin, remembering Mr. Goon's words of warning about the five children, looked at him rather doubtfully. This wasn't the dangerous fat boy, though—it was one of the others.

'Good morning, Mr. Pippin,' said Larry, politely. 'Settled in all right?'

'Of course,' said Mr. Pippin. 'Nice place, Peterswood. I've always liked it. You at home for the Easter holidays?'

'Yes,' said Larry. 'Er—got on to any mystery yet, Mr. Pippin?'

'Shouldn't tell you if I had,' said Mr. Pippin, grinning at Larry. 'I've had a Warning about you, see?'

'Yes. We thought you probably would have,' said Larry. 'By the way, our cook had a fright last night. Said she saw two ruffians outside our back door.'

Mr. Pippin pricked up his ears at once. 'Did she? What were they like?'

'Well—she said one of them had red hair,' said Larry. 'But you'd better ask her if you want any particulars. Why? Have *you* seen them?'

'Perhaps I have and perhaps I haven't,' said Mr. Pippin, annoyingly.

3

He nodded to Larry and walked off. He was thinking hard. So Larry's cook had also seen a red-haired ruffian. Must have been the same red-haired fellow that he too had seen that night then. What were they up to ? He decided to interview Larry's cook, and did so. He came away with a very lurid account of two enormous villains, six feet high at least, growling and groaning, squinting and pulling faces.

One of them certainly had red hair. Mr. Pippin began to look out for people with red hair. When he met Mr. Kerry the cobbler, who had flaming red hair, he eyed him with such suspicion that Mr. Kerry felt really alarmed.

P.C. Pippin also came across the vicar's brother, a kind and harmless tricyclist who liked to ride three times round the village each morning for exercise. When Mr. Pippin had met him for the third time, and scrutinized him very very carefully, the vicar's brother began to think something must be wrong. Mr. Pippin was also surprised—how many more times was he going to see this red-haired tricyclist ?

When Larry related to the others that he had met Pippin, and told him about the red-haired man seen by the cook, and when Fatty heard from Janet the cook that the policeman had actually been to interview her about him, he chuckled.

'I think a spot of disguising is indicated,' he said to the others. 'A few red-haired fellows might interest our nice round ripe Pippin.'

So at twelve o'clock a red-haired telegraph boy appeared on a bicycle, whistling piercingly. When he saw Mr. Pippin he stopped and asked him to

direct him to an address he didn't know. The
policeman looked at him. Another red-haired
fellow ! There was no end to them in Peterswood,
it seemed.

At half-past one another red-haired fellow
appeared beside the surprised Pippin. This time
he was a man with a basket. He had black eyebrows
which looked rather odd with his red hair, and
frightful teeth that stuck out in front. He talked
badly because of these.

'Scuthe me,' lisped the red-haired fellow.
"Pleathe, can you thay where the Potht Offith ith ?'

At first P.C. Pippin thought the fellow was
talking in a foreign language, but at last discovered
that he was merely lisping. He looked at him
closely. *Another* red-haired chap ! Most peculiar.
None of them really looked like the ruffian he had
seen the night before, though.

At half-past two yet another red-haired fellow
knocked at P.C. Pippin's door, and delivered a
newspaper which he said must have been left at the
wrong house. Pippin thought it was one that Goon
had, and thanked him. He stared at him, frowning.
All this red hair ! Fatty stared back unwinkingly.

Feeling uncomfortable, though he didn't know
why, P.C. Pippin shut the door and went back into
the front room. He felt that if he saw one more
red-haired man that day he would really go to the
occulist and see if there was something wrong with
his eyes !

And at half-past five, when he was setting out to
go to the post, what did he see but an elderly looking
man shuffling along with a stick—and with bright-
red hair sticking out from under his cap !

' I'm seeing things,' thought poor Mr. Pippin to himself. ' I've got red hair on the brain.'

Then a memory struck him. ' Well ! What was it that Mr. Goon told me ? He warned me against red-headed fellows dashing about all over the place, didn't he ? What did he mean ? What's all this red-haired business ? Oh yes—Mr. Goon said it would be Fatty disguising himself ! But that boy *couldn't* be as clever as all that ! ' Mr. Pippin began to review all the red-haired people he had seen that day. He thought with especial suspicion of the man he had seen three times on a tricycle.

' Ah ! Wait till I meet the next red-head,' said Mr. Pippin darkly to himself. ' If there's tricks played on *me*, I can play a few too ! I'll give the next red-head a Real Fright ! '

It so happened that the next one he met was the vicar's brother on his tricycle again, hurrying along to catch the post at the post office. Mr. Pippin stepped out into the road in front of him.

The vicar's brother rang his bell violently but Mr. Pippin didn't get out of the way. So the rider put on his brakes suddenly, and came to such a sudden stop that he almost fell off.

' What is it, constable ? ' said the vicar's brother, astonished. ' I nearly ran you down.'

' What's your name and address, please ? ' asked Mr. Pippin, taking out his note-book.

' My name is Theodore Twit, and my address is the Vicarage,' said Mr. Twit, with much dignity.

' Ho *yes*,' said Mr. Pippin. " The Vicarage " I *don't* think ! You can't put me off *that* way ! '

Mr. Twit wondered if the policeman was mad.

He looked at him anxiously. Mr. Pippin mistook his anxious look for fright. He suddenly clutched at Mr. Twit's abundant, red hair.

' Ow ! ' said Mr. Twit, and almost overbalanced from his tricycle. ' Constable ! What does this mean ? '

Mr. Pippin had been absolutely certain that the red hair would come off in his hand. When it didn't, he was horrified. He stared at Mr. Twit, his pink face going a deep red.

' Do you feel all right, constable ? ' asked Mr. Twit, rubbing his head where Mr. Pippin had snatched at his hair. ' I don't understand you. Oh—thank goodness, here is my sister. Muriel, do come here and tell this constable who I am. He doesn't seem to believe me.'

Mr. Pippin saw a large and very determined-looking lady coming towards him. ' What is it, Theodore ? ' said the lady, in a deep, barking kind of voice. Mr. Pippin took one look at Muriel, muttered a few words of shamed apology, and fled. He left behind him two very puzzled people.

' Mad,' said Muriel, in her barking voice. ' Goon was mad enough, goodness knows—but really when it comes to this man snatching at your hair, Theodore, the world must be coming to an end ! '

It so happened that Miss Twit went to call on Fatty's mother that evening, and when Fatty heard her relate the story of how that extraordinary Mr. Pippin had tried to snatch at dear Theodore's red hair, he had such a fit of the giggles that his mother sent him out of the room in disgust at his manners. Fatty enjoyed his laugh all to himself, with Buster gazing at him in wonder.

' So old Pippin is up to that trick, is he ? ' thought Fatty. ' Right. It must be dropped. Hope he doesn't associate me with the red-haired ruffian he saw last night, though. He won't turn up at the Little Theatre and find his precious Clues if he thinks it's a trick.'

The five children had had a meeting that day, which was Thursday, to decide what clues they would spread for Pippin at the back of the Little Theatre. There was a kind of verandah there, under cover, where all kinds of clues might be put.

' Cigarette-ends, of course, to make Pippin think other meetings have taken place there,' said Fatty.

' Yes—and matches,' said Larry. ' And what about a hanky with an initial on it—always very helpful that, when you want clues ! '

' Oh yes,' said Daisy. ' I've got an old torn hanky and I'll work an initial on it. What shall I put ?

' Z,' said Fatty, promptly. ' Might as well give him something to puzzle his brains over.'

' Z ! ' said Bets. ' But there aren't any names beginning with Z, surely.'

' Yes there are—Zebediah and Zacharias, to start with ! ' grinned Fatty. ' We'll have old Pippin hunting round for Zebediahs before he's very much older ! '

' Well, I'll put a Z on then,' said Daisy. ' I'll get my needle and thread now. What other clues will you put down ? '

' A page out of a book,' said Pip. ' Out of a time-table or something.'

' Yes. That's good,' said Fatty, approvingly. ' Any other ideas ? '

'What else do people drop by accident?' wondered Daisy. 'Oh, I know what we could do. If there's a nail or anything there, we could take along a bit of cloth and jab it on the nail! Then it would look as if whoever had been there for a meeting had caught his coat on the nail. That would be a very valuable clue, if it was a real one!'

'Yes, it would,' agreed Fatty. 'And we'll take a pencil and sharpen it there—leave bits of pencil-shavings all over the place. Gosh, what a wonderful lot of clues!'

'We must also leave something to make Pippin go on with the chase somewhere else,' said Larry.

'Yes. What about underlining a train in the time-table page that we're going to throw down?' said Pip. 'We're going to chuck one down, aren't we? Well, if we underline a certain train—say a Sunday train—old Pippin will turn up for that too!'

Every one giggled. 'And Fatty could dress up in some disguise, and slip a message into Pippin's hand to suggest the next place to go to,' said Daisy. 'We could send him half over the country at this rate!'

'Wait till Goon gets a report of all this,' said Fatty with a grin. 'He'll see through it at once—and won't he be wild!'

Soon all the clues were ready, even to the pencil-shavings, which were in an envelope.

'When shall we place the clues?' said Bets. 'Can I come too?'

'Yes. We'll all go,' said Fatty. 'I don't see why not. There's nothing suspicious about us all going out together. We can go on our bicycles and

put them in the car-park at the back of the Little
Theatre. Then we'll pretend to be looking at the
posters there, and one of us can slip up to the
verandah and park the clues. It won't take a
minute.'

'When shall we go?' asked Bets again. She
always wanted to do things at once.

'Not to-day,' said Fatty. 'There's a bit of a
breeze. We don't want the clues blown right off the
verandah. The wind may have died down by to-
morrow. We'll cycle along after tea to-morrow,
about six.'

So the next day, about ten to six, the five set off,
with Buster as usual in Fatty's bicycle basket. They
cycled round to the back of the Little Theatre and
came to the car-park there. A good many children
were there already, getting bicycles from the
stand.

'Hallo!' said Fatty, surprised. 'Has there been
a show here this afternoon?'

'Yes,' said a boy near by. 'Just a show for us
children from Farleigh Homes. They let us in for
nothing. It was jolly good. I liked the cat the
best.'

'The cat? Oh, Dick Whittington's cat, you
mean,' said Fatty, remembering that the show that
week was supposed to be a skit on the Dick Whittington pantomime. 'It's not a real cat, is it?'

''Course not!' said the boy. Daisy, who had
already seen the show, explained to Fatty.

'It's a man in a cat's skin, idiot. Must be rather
a small man—or maybe it's a boy! He was very
funny, I thought.'

'Look—there go the actors,' said a little girl,

and she pointed to a side door. ' See, that's Dick
Whittington, that pretty girl. Why do they always
have a girl for the boy in a pantomime? And that's
Margot, who is Dick's sweetheart in the play. And
there's Dick's master—and his mother, look—she's
a man, really, as you can see. And there's the captain
of Dick's ship—isn't he fine? And there's the chief
of the islands that Dick visits—only in the play he's
a black man, of course.'

The five children gazed at the actors as they
left the side door of the Little Theatre. They all
looked remarkably ordinary.

' Where's the cat? ' asked Bets.

' He doesn't seem to have gone with them,'
said the little girl. ' Anyway I wouldn't know what
he was like, because he wore his cat-skin all the time.
He was awfully good. I loved him.'

A teacher called loudly, ' Irene! Donald! What
are you keeping us waiting for? Come along at
once.'

The car-park emptied. Fatty looked round.
' Now,' he said, ' come on! The coast is clear.
We'll all go and look at these posters here, and talk
to one another—and then when we are sure no one
is watching us, I'll slip up to the verandah and drop
the clues.'

It was most annoying, however, because one or
two people kept coming to the car-park, and for some
reason or other walked across it. Fatty finally
discovered that it was a short cut to a cigarette shop
in the next street.

' Blow! ' he said. ' We'll have to hang about
till it shuts. It's sure to shut soon.'

It was boring having to wait so long, and talk

endlessly about the posters. But at last the shop apparently did shut and nobody else took the short cut across the car-park. It was now getting dark. Fatty slipped up the three steps to the verandah.

He threw down the clues—cigarette-ends and matches—torn hanky with Z on—pencil-shavings— page torn from a time-table with one Sunday train underlined—and a bit of navy-blue cloth which he jabbed hard on a nail.

He turned to go—but before he went he took a look in at the window near by. And what a shock Fatty got !

V. P.C. PIPPIN ON THE JOB

A VERY large, furry animal was inside the window, looking mournfully up at him—or so it seemed. The eyes were big and glassy, and gave Fatty the creeps. He recoiled back from the window, and almost fell down the verandah steps.

'What's up?' asked Larry, surprised.

'There's something queer up there,' said Fatty. 'Horrible big animal, looking out of the window at me. I could just see it in the faint reflection cast by that street-lamp outside the car-park.'

Bets gave a little squeal. 'Don't! I'm frightened!'

'Idiot, Fatty! It must be the cat-skin of Dick Whittington's cat,' said Larry, after a moment. Every one felt most relieved.

'Well—I suppose it was,' said Fatty, feeling very foolish. 'I never thought of that. The thing looked so lifelike, though. I don't think it was just a *skin*. I think the actor who plays the cat must have still been inside it.'

'Gracious. Does he *live* in it, then?' said Daisy. 'Let's go and see if it's still there, looking out of the window.'

'I don't want to,' said Bets at once.

'I don't think I do either, really,' said Daisy.

'*We'll* go,' said Larry. 'Come on, Fatty, come on, Pip.'

The three boys stepped quietly up the verandah steps, and looked in at the window. The cat was no longer there, but as they stood watching, they saw it come in at the door of the room and run across on all fours to the fireplace. An electric fire was burning, and the boys could distinctly see the cat pretending to wash its face, rubbing its ears with its paws, in exactly the same way as a cat does.

' There it is ! ' said Fatty. ' It's seen us ! That's why it's acting up like this. It thinks we're children who came to see the show, and it's still pretending to be Dick Whittington's Cat. Gracious—it gave me a start when I first saw it at the window.'

' Meeow,' said the cat, loudly, turning towards the window, and waving a paw.

' I somehow don't like it,' said Pip. ' I don't know why. But I just don't. I know it's only somebody inside the skin, but it looks a jolly sight too real for me. Let's go ! '

They went back to the girls. It was now quite dark, and the church clock struck seven o'clock as they went to fetch their bicycles from the stands.

' Well—we've planted the clues,' said Fatty, feeling more cheerful as he undid Buster from where he had tied him to the stand. ' I say, Buster, old chap—good thing you didn't spot that cat. You'd have thought you were seeing things—a cat as big as that ! '

' Woof,' said Buster, dolefully. He didn't like being left out of the fun, and he knew something exciting had been happening. He was lifted into Fatty's basket, and then the five cycled slowly home.

' I wonder when Pippin will go along,' said Fatty, as he dismounted at his gate. ' He'll be sure to get there long before ten, so that he can hide before the meeting takes place—and there won't be a meeting after all ! Only plenty of clues for him to find.'

' See you to-morrow, Fatty ! ' called Pip and Bets. ' Good-bye, Larry and Daisy. We'll have to hurry or we'll get into a row.'

They all rode away. Fatty went indoors, thinking of the way the cat had looked at him through the window. That really had given him a jolt! ' If I were Bets I'd dream about that ! ' he thought. ' I wonder if Pippin's going to hide himself on the verandah somewhere. If he gets a glimpse of that cat, he'll get the fright of his life.'

Pippin did not go to the verandah until about half-past eight. He meant to be there in good time for the meeting, whatever it was. He had been very thrilled indeed to find the message about the meeting at 10 p.m. behind the Little Theatre, when he had pieced together the torn bits of paper.

Goon would be pleased with him if he could unearth some mystery or plot, he was sure. Pippin meant to do his best. He had already snooped round the back of the Little Theatre the day before, to see where he could hide on the night. He had discovered a hole in the verandah roof through which he could climb, and then he could sit on the window-sill of the room above, and hear everything.

Pippin arrived at the verandah as the clock on the church chimed half-past eight, exactly an hour and a half after the children had left. He had his torch with him, but did not put it on until he had made sure that there was nobody about anywhere. There was a glow in the room behind the verandah. Pippin looked into the room. He saw that the glow came from an electric fire. In front of it, lying as if

asleep, was what looked like a most enormous cat.
Pippin jumped violently when he saw such a big
creature.

He couldn't believe his eyes. *Was* it a cat?
Yes—there were its ears—and there was its tail
lying beside it on the hearth-rug.

Pippin gazed into the window at the great, furry
creature outlined by the glow of the fire. It couldn't
be a gorilla, could it? No, people wouldn't be
allowed to keep a gorilla like that. Besides, it looked
more like a cat than anything else.

Pippin was just about to give a loud exclamation
when he stopped himself in time. Of course! It
must be Dick Whittington's Cat—the one that
acted in the skit in the pantomime. He hadn't
seen it himself, but he had heard about it. Funny
the cat keeping its skin on like that—because it was
really somebody inside it. You'd think he'd want
to take the hot skin off as soon as he could!

Pippin wondered if the meeting, whatever it was,
would take place if there was that cat in the room
near by. But perhaps the meeting would be in the
car-park. In that case would it be much good him
climbing up on the verandah roof? He wouldn't
hear a thing.

Pippin debated with himself. He cautiously
switched on his torch and flashed it round the
verandah floor. And he saw the clues!

His eyes brightened as he saw the cigarette-ends,
the matches, and the pencil-shavings. Somebody
had been here before—quite often too, judging by
the cigarette-ends. The verandah must certainly be
the meeting-place. Perhaps the cat was in the plot
too. That was certainly an idea!

Carefully Pippin picked up the cigarette-ends, the matches, and even the pencil shavings. He put them all into envelopes. He then found the torn time-table page, blown against the side of the verandah, and was extremely interested in the underlined Sunday train.

He looked round and found the handkerchief with Z on it, and wondered if it could be the letter N sideways. Pippin could not for the life of him think of any name beginning with Z, not even the ones the children had thought of !

Then he spotted the bit of navy-blue cloth caught on a nail. Aha ! Oho ! *That* was the most valuable clue of all. Find somebody with a hole in a navy-blue coat and you were getting somewhere !

Pippin took another cautious look into the window of the room at the back of the verandah. The great cat was still lying in front of the electric fire. Very strange—especially if you considered that the cat wasn't really a cat but a human being inside a cat-skin—or a furry skin of some sort. As he watched, Pippin saw the cat move a little, get more comfortable and apparently settle itself to sleep again.

' Funny creature,' thought Pippin, still puzzled, but very much relieved to see the cat move. ' I sort of feel if a mouse ran across the room, the cat would be after it—though I know it's not a real cat ! '

He decided that it was quite time he climbed up through the hole in the verandah roof, and sat on the window-sill of the room above. The men might come at any moment now—one of them might be early—you never knew ! It wouldn't do for him to be seen.

With all his clues safely in his pocket Pippin

heaved himself up through the hole in the roof. He felt his way to the window-sill and sat down on it. It was hard and cold, and much too narrow to be comfortable. Pippin resigned himself to a long and uneasy wait.

He had not been there more than a few moments when he heard a very queer sound. Pippin stiffened and listened. It sounded to him very like a groan. But where could it be coming from ? The room behind him was in black darkness. There was nobody near him out of doors as far as he knew— and if it was the cat before the fire making a noise, how could he *possibly* hear that ? He couldn't !

The noise came again, and Pippin felt most peculiar. There he was, sitting on a narrow window-sill in the dark, waiting for rogues to meet down below—and groans sounding all round him ! He didn't like it at all.

He listened, holding his breath. The groan came again. It was *behind* him ! Pippin suddenly felt sure of that. Well, then, it must be in the *room* behind him ! Pippin felt round the window, meaning to open it. But it was shut and fastened from inside.

Pippin remembered his torch. He took it from his belt and switched it on, so that the light shone into the room behind. Its beam swung slowly round the room—and then came to rest on something very queer.

A man was sitting at a desk. He had fallen forward, his face on his out-stretched arms. Beside him was a cup, overturned in its saucer, the spoon nearby on the table. Pippin stared in horror.

Then the beam picked out something else. A

A MAN WAS SITTING AT A DESK.

big wall-mirror was standing on the floor, reflecting the light of the torch.   A large hole showed in the wall near by, the place from which the mirror had been removed.   A safe had been built in behind the mirror—but it was now empty, and the safe-door was swinging open.

'Thieves!   A robbery!' said P.C. Pippin, and rose to the occasion at once.   He doubled his hand in folds of his big handkerchief and drove his fist through the window !   P.C. Pippin was on the job !

VI. A MYSTERY BEGINS

THE five children knew nothing about P.C. Pippin's exciting night, of course. Pip and Bets were asleep in bed when he smashed the window at the back of the Little Theatre, and Larry and Daisy had been told they could listen to the nine o'clock news, and then go to bed. Fatty had been in his room trying out a wonderful new Aid to Disguise—little pads to put inside the cheeks and make them fat!

'I'll try these to-morrow,' thought Fatty, with a grin. 'I'll put them in before breakfast and see if any one notices.'

Fatty went to bed wondering if P.C. Pippin had found the clues he had spread about the verandah, and how long he had waited for the mythical meeting. Poor old Pippin—he might have waited a long time!

If Fatty had only known what was happening he would never have gone off so peacefully to bed that night—he would have been snooping round the Little Theatre, looking for *real* Clues! But all he had done was to play a trick on P.C. Pippin that had placed that gentleman right on the Spot—the very Spot where a burglary had taken place not so long before. Lucky Pippin!

Next day at breakfast Fatty put in his new Aid to Disguise—the cheek-pads that forced out the soft part of his cheeks and made him look plumper than ever. His father, buried behind his paper, didn't seem to notice any difference. He always thought Fatty was too plump anyhow. But his mother was puzzled. Fatty looked different. What was it that made him look strange? It was his cheeks! They were quite blown out.

'Frederick—have you got toothache?' suddenly asked his mother. 'Your cheeks are very swollen.'

'Oh no, Mother,' said Fatty. 'My teeth are quite all right.'

'Well, you don't seem to be eating as much as usual, which is very queer, and certainly your cheeks look swollen,' persisted his mother. 'I shall ring up and make an appointment with the dentist.'

This was really very alarming. Fatty didn't want the dentist poking round his mouth and finding holes in his teeth. He felt quite certain that even if there wasn't a hole the dentist would make one with that nasty scrapey instrument of his.

'Mother—do believe me—not one of my teeth has holes in,' said Fatty, desperately. 'I ought to know.'

'Well, then, why are your cheeks so puffed out?' asked his mother, who never could leave a subject alone once she had really started on it. She turned to his father. 'Don't *you* think Frederick's cheeks are swollen?'

His father glanced up in an absent-minded manner. 'Always does look too fat,' he said. 'Eats too much.' Then to Fatty's relief he went on reading his newspaper.

'I'll ring up the dentist immediately after breakfast,' said Fatty's mother.

In desperation Fatty put his hands to his mouth and removed the two cheek-pads—but instead of being pleased that his cheeks were now no longer swollen, his mother cried out in disgust. 'Frederick! How *can* you behave like that! Removing food from your mouth with your fingers ! What *is* the matter with you this morning ? You'd better leave the table.'

Before Fatty could explain about the cheek-pads, his father gave an exclamation. 'Well, well ! Listen to this in the paper. " Last night it was disclosed that the manager of the Little Theatre, in Peterswood, Bucks., was found drugged in his office, and the safe in the wall behind him was open, the contents having been stolen. The police already have one suspect in their hands." '

Fatty was so astounded to hear this that he absent-mindedly put his cheek-pads into his mouth, thinking they were bits of bread, and began to chew them. He simply couldn't believe the news. Why, he and the others had actually been hanging round the Little Theatre half the evening, and they had seen nothing at all—except the Pantomime Cat !

'Could I see the piece, Dad ? ' asked Fatty, wondering why the bread in his mouth was so tough. He suddenly realized that it wasn't bread—ugh, how horrible, he had been chewing his cheek-pads ! And now he didn't dare to remove them again in case his mother accused him of disgusting manners once more. It was very awkward.

'Don't talk with your mouth full, Frederick,' said his mother. 'And of course you can't have your father's paper. You can read it when he has finished with it.'

Very fortunately at that moment the telephone bell rang. The house-parlourmaid answered it and came to fetch Fatty's mother. So Fatty was able to remove the half-chewed cheek-pads and put them into his pocket. He decided never to wear them again at meal-times. He glanced longingly at his father's paper. Ah—he had folded it over again and the bit about the robbery was on the back, but upside down. Fatty managed to read it two or three times. He began to feel very excited.

Would it be a Mystery? Suppose they hadn't got the right Suspect? Then the Five Find-Outers could get on to it at once. Fatty felt that he couldn't possibly eat any more breakfast. He slid away quietly from the table before his mother came back. His father didn't notice him go.

Fatty flew off to Pip's at once. Larry and Daisy would be along soon, for they had planned a meeting there. Pip and Bets had a fine big playroom of their own, where they were not often disturbed, and it made a very good meeting-place.

Pip and Bets had heard nothing of the great news. Fatty told them, and they were amazed. 'What! A robbery committed last night at the Little Theatre! Did it happen whilst we were there?' cried Pip, in excitement. 'Here's Larry, with Daisy. I say, Larry, heard the news about the Little Theatre Robbery?'

Larry and Daisy had heard all about it. They knew even more than Fatty because Janet, their cook, knew the woman who cleaned the Little Theatre, and had got some news from her, which she had passed on to Larry and Daisy. Larry said Janet felt certain that the robbers were the two ruffians she had seen the other night in the beam of light from the kitchen door!

'To think we were all there last evening, mooching round, hanging about and everything!' groaned Fatty. 'And we never saw a thing. We were so busy preparing clues for old Pippin that we never saw anything of a real crime that must have been going on almost under our noses.'

'Janet says that Mrs. Trotter, the woman who cleans the Little Theatre, told her that last night the police found the manager stretched out across his office desk, his head on his arms, asleep from some drug—and behind him was his empty safe,' said Larry. ' It was one that was built in the wall, hidden by a big wall-mirror hanging in front of it. She said the police must have discovered the whole thing not very long after it was done.'

' The police ! I suppose that means P.C. Pippin,' said Fatty. ' Gosh—to think we planted him there on that verandah, surrounded by a whole lot of false clues—and there he was right on the spot when a real robbery was committed ! It's absolutely maddening. If only we'd snooped round a bit more, *we* might have hit on the mystery ourselves. As it is, we've presented it to the police—or rather to P.C. Pippin—and they will get in straight away, and solve the whole thing.'

There was a doleful silence. It did seem very hard luck.

' I suppose Pippin will think all those cigarette-ends and hanky and so on are real clues now—clues to the real robbers, I mean,' said Bets, after a long pause.

' Gosh ! So he will ! He'll be right off on the wrong track,' said Fatty. ' That's awkward. Very awkward. I don't mind playing a silly trick on either Goon or Pippin—but I wouldn't want to do anything that would prevent them from catching the burglars. Those clues of ours will certainly fog them a bit.'

'You mean—they'll start looking for people whose names begin with Z, and they'll go and watch that Sunday train?' said Daisy. 'Instead of going on the right trail.'

'Yes,' said Fatty. 'Well—I think I'd better go and see P.C. Pippin, and own up. I don't want to set him off on the wrong track—make him waste his time solving a pretend mystery when he's got a real one to see to. Blow! It will be very awkward, having to explain. And I bet he won't give me any information, either, because he'll be so annoyed with me for playing a trick on him. We could have worked in nicely with old Pippin. We never could work with Goon.'

Every one felt very glum. To think they had gone and spoilt a perfectly super *real* mystery by making up a stupid pretend one!

'I'll come with you to explain,' said Larry.

'No,' said Fatty. 'I take the responsibility for this. I'd like to keep the rest of you out of it—if Pippin takes it into his head to complain of us, my parents won't take a lot of notice—but yours will, Larry—and as for Pip's parents, they'll go right off the deep end.'

'They always do,' said Pip. His parents were very strict with him and Bets, and had been very much annoyed three or four times already when Mr. Goon had complained to them about the children. 'I don't want our parents to know a thing. Mother's already said she's glad Goon is away because now perhaps we won't get into any mischief these holidays, and make Goon come round and grumble about us.'

'I'll go and see Pippin now,' said Fatty, getting

up. 'Nothing like getting a nasty thing done at
once. I do hope Pippin won't mind too much.
Actually I think he's rather nice. He'll be thrilled
at getting a case like this when Goon is away.'

He went out, with Buster close at his heels.
He whistled loudly to show that he didn't care
about anything in the world. But actually Fatty
did care quite a lot this morning. He felt guilty
about all those false clues. He could have kicked
himself for spoiling his chance of working in with
P.C. Pippin. Pippin wasn't like Goon. He looked
sensible, and Fatty felt sure he would have welcomed
his, Fatty's, help.

He came to Goon's house, in which Pippin was
now living whilst Goon was away. To his surprise
the door was wide open. Fatty walked in to find
Pippin.

There was a loud voice talking in the front
room. Fatty stopped as if he had been shot. It
was Goon's voice. *Goon!* Had he come back then?
Was he going to take over the mystery? Blow!

Fatty stood there, wondering what to do. He
wasn't going to confess to Pippin in front of Goon!
That would be very, very foolish. Goon might even
take it into his head to go and tell Inspector Jenks,
the children's very great friend—and somehow
Fatty felt that the Inspector would not approve of
the little trick they had played on the unsuspecting
Pippin.

Goon was evidently very angry. His voice was
raised, and he was going for poor Pippin unmerci-
fully. Fatty couldn't help hearing, as he stood in
the passage, undecided whether to go in or out.

'Why didn't you send for me when you first saw

those rogues under that bush in the garden ? Why didn't you tell me about the torn-up note ? Didn't I tell you to let me know if anything happened ? Turnip-head ! Dolt ! Soon as I go away they put in a dud like you, who hasn't even got the sense to send for his superior when something happens ! '

Fatty decided to go—but Buster decided differently. Aha ! That was the voice of his old enemy, wasn't it ? With a joyful bark Buster pushed open the door of the sitting-room with his black nose, and bounded in !

VII. GOON—PIPPIN—AND FATTY

THERE was a loud exclamation from Goon. 'That dog! Where did it come from? Clear-orf, you! Ah, you'd nip me in the ankles, would you!'

Fatty rushed into the room at once, afraid that Goon would hurt Buster. Pippin was standing by the window, looking very crestfallen indeed. Goon was by the fireplace, kicking out at Buster, who was dancing happily round his feet.

Goon looked up and saw Fatty. 'Oh, you're here too, are you?' he said. 'Setting your dog on me again! What with having to deal with that turnip-head over there, and this dratted dog, and you, it's enough to make a man retire from the police force!'

To Fatty's horror he caught up the poker and hit Buster with it on the back. Buster gave a howl of pain. Fatty ran to Goon and twisted the poker out of his hand. The boy was white with fury.

'See?' said Goon, turning to Pippin, who was also looking rather white. 'See that? You're a witness, you are—that boy sets his dog on me, and when I protect myself, as I've a right to do, the boy comes and assaults me. You're a witness, Pippin. Write it all down. Go on. I've been after this pest of a boy and his dog for a long time—and now I've got him. You saw it all, didn't you, Pippin?'

Fatty now had Buster in his arms. He could not trust himself to speak. He knew Goon to be a stupid, ignorant man with a turn for cruelty, but

Goon had never shown his real nature quite so openly before.

Pippin said nothing at all. He stood by the window, looking scared and very much taken-aback. He had been shouted at by Goon for half an hour, blamed for all kinds of things, called all kinds of names—and now he was supposed to take out his note-book and put down a lot of untruths about that nice dog and his master.

' Pippin ! Will you please write down what I tell you ? ' stormed Goon. ' I'll have that dog destroyed. I'll have this boy up before the court. I'll . . ."

Buster growled so fiercely that Goon stopped. ' Look here,' said Fatty, ' if you're going to do all that, I think I'll put Buster down and let him have a real good go at you, Goon. He may as well be hanged for a sheep as for a lamb. He hasn't bitten you, as you very well know—but if you're going to say he has, well then, he jolly well *can*.'

And Fatty made as if he was going to put the barking, struggling Buster down on the floor !

Goon calmed down at once, and tried to get back control of himself. He turned in a dignified way to Pippin. ' I'll tell you what to put down. Come on now, stir yourself—standing there like a ninny ! '

' I'm not going to put down anything but the truth,' said Pippin, most surprisingly. ' You hit that dog a nasty whack with the poker—might have injured him for life. I don't hold with behaviour of that sort, no, not even from a police officer. I like dogs—they never go for *me*. I wouldn't have that dog destroyed for anything. And all the boy did was to take the poker from you to stop you hitting his dog again ! A good thing he did too. You might have killed the dog with your next whack— and then where would you be ? In a very awkward position, Mr. Goon, that's where ! '

There was a dead silence after this unexpected and remarkable speech. Even Buster was quiet. Every one was most surprised to hear this speech from the quiet Pippin, and perhaps Pippin himself was most surprised of all. Goon couldn't believe his ears. He stared at Pippin with his mouth wide open, and his eyes bulged more than ever. Fatty was thrilled. Good old Pippin !

Goon found his tongue at last. His face was now a familiar purple. He advanced to Pippin and shook a fat and rather dirty finger under his nose.

' You'll hear more of this, see ? I'm back again and I'm in charge of Peterswood now. *I'll* take charge of this new case—and you'll have nothing to do with it whatever. Nothing. If you thought you'd get a good mark for it from the Inspector you can think again. I'll make a bad report out on you and your behaviour—thinking you'd manage it by yourself and get all the praise—not letting me know anything. Gah ! '

Pippin said nothing, but looked thoroughly miserable. Fatty was very sorry for him. Goon was enjoying ticking off Pippin in front of Fatty. It gave him a sense of power, and he loved that.

' You hand me over all them clues,' said Goon. ' Every one of them. Aha ! Master Frederick Trotteville would very much like to know what they are—wouldn't you ? But you won't know ! You'll never know ! '

Pippin handed over to Mr. Goon all the false

clues that Fatty had put on the verandah ! They
were in envelopes or paper so Fatty could not see
them—but he knew very well what they were !
In fact he could have given Goon quite a lot of
information about them. He grinned to himself.
Right ! Let Goon have them and work on them.
Much good would they do him ! Served him right
for being so beastly to Pippin.

‘ See what happens to people who work against
me, instead of with me ? ’ said Goon to Fatty,
spitefully. ‘ I shan’t let him have anything to do
with this new case—and you kids won’t neither !
I’ll manage it myself. Pippin, you can do my
routine work the next two weeks, and keep your
nose out of anything else. I don’t want your help
—not that a turnip-head like you could help a
fellow like me. Don’t you come mewling to me with
any of your silly ideas—I just don’t want to hear
them.’

He put away all the clues in a box and locked it.
‘ Now I’m going along to interview the manager of
the Little Theatre,’ he said. ‘ Ho yes, I know
you’ve interviewed him already, Mister Clever—
but I don’t care tuppence for what you’ve got out
of him—it won’t be anything worth while. Well,
you get down to that writing I ticked you off about
—and just remember this—I shan’t forget your
insubordination this morning over that there pestiferous dog. Yes, real, right-down insubordination
—refusal to perform your rightful duties when
commanded. Gah ! ’

Mr. Goon made a dignified and haughty departure,
walking ponderously down the path to his front
gate, and shutting it sharply. Fatty, Buster, and

'YOU'LL HEAR MORE OF THIS, SEE? I'M BACK AGAIN AND I'M
IN CHARGE OF PETERSWOOD NOW.'

Pippin were left together in the little sitting-room.
Fatty put Buster down. He at once ran to Pippin
and pawed eagerly at his legs, whining.

Pippin stooped down and patted him. He
looked so miserable that Fatty wanted to comfort
him.

' He's thanking you for sticking up for him,'
he said. ' Thanks from me, too, Mr. Pippin. Awfully decent of you.'

' He's a nice dog,' said Pippin. ' I like dogs.
I've got one of my own, back home. Goon wouldn't
let me bring him here.'

' I bet you think just about the same of Goon
as I do—as we all do,' said Fatty. ' He's a beast.
Always has been. He'd no right to speak to you in
that way, you know.'

' I thought I was on to such a good case,' said
Pippin, sitting down and taking out his fountain
pen to write. ' I was going to send for Goon this
morning, of course—but he saw a notice in the
paper and came tearing back, accusing me of not
having told him anything. Now I've had to give
him all my clues—and he'll use them instead of me.'

Fatty considered things carefully. Should he
confess to Pippin now that they were not real clues ?
No—Goon had them—let him mess about with
them ! Fatty thought that possibly Pippin might
feel he ought to tell Goon they were false clues, if he,
Fatty, confessed to him that they were—and that
would spoil everything. Goon would go and complain to their parents, they would be forbidden to
try and solve this mystery, and Pippin would be
called over the coals by Goon for being so stupid
as to be taken in by false clues.

It would be very nice indeed if Goon would busy himself with those clues, and leave the way clear for Fatty and the other Find-Outers to go to work! Pippin might help them. That would be better still.

'Mr. Pippin, don't take any notice of what Mr. Goon says to you,' said Fatty, earnestly. 'I am sure that Inspector Jenks, who is a great friend of ours, wouldn't allow him to speak to you like that, if he knew.'

'The Inspector told me about you and the others,' said Pippin. 'He's got a very high opinion of you, I must say. Said you'd been no end of a help in solving all kinds of mysterious cases.'

Fatty saw his chance and took it. 'Yes—that's true—and, Pippin, I shall be on to this case too—and probably solve it! I should be very proud if you would help us—it would be nice to present the Inspector with another mystery correctly solved. He'd be thrilled.'

Pippin looked up at the earnest Fatty. Fatty was only a boy in his teens, but there was something about him that made people respect him and trust him. Brains? Yes. Character? Plenty! Cheek? Too much. Pluck? Any amount. Pippin saw all this as he looked at Fatty and sized him up. Well—if Inspector Jenks liked this boy and admired him, then he, Pippin, was quite prepared to do the same —very willing to, in fact, seeing that it looked as if Fatty was not going to work with Mr. Goon! Pippin couldn't help thinking it would be very nice indeed to help this boy to solve the mystery—what a sell for Mr. Goon that would be!

'Well,' he said, and paused. 'Well—I'd like
5

to help you—but wouldn't I have to tell Mr. Goon anything we discovered ? '

' But, Mr. Pippin, didn't you hear him tell you that he didn't want your help ? ' said Fatty. ' Didn't you hear him say you weren't to go to him with any of your silly mewling ideas—whatever *they* are ! You'd be disobeying his orders if you told him anything.'

This seemed a very sensible way out to Pippin. Yes—he certainly would be disobeying orders if he went and told Mr. Goon anything now. On the other hand, surely it was his duty to work on the case if he could. Wasn't he the one to discover the robbery ?

' I'll help you,' he told Fatty, and the boy grinned with pleasure. ' I guess if the Inspector has let you meddle in other cases, he'd say you could meddle in this one too. Anyway—I'd like to pay Goon back for some of the beastly things he said to me.'

' Hear, hear—very human and natural of you,' said Fatty, agreeing heartily. ' Well now, Pippin, I'll lay my cards on the table—and you can lay yours there as well. I'll tell you all I know, and you can tell me all *you* know.'

' What do *you* know ? ' said Pippin, curiously.

' Well—I and the other four were round at the back of the Little Theatre from about half-past five last night till seven,' said Fatty. ' Just snooping about, you know—looking at the posters and things.'

' Oh, you were, were you ? ' said Pippin, sitting up and taking notice. ' Did you see anything interesting ? '

' I looked in at the window at the back of that

verandah,' said Fatty. 'And I saw the Pantomime
Cat there—at least, I feel sure that's what it must
have been. It was like a huge furry cat. It came to
the window and stared at me—gave me an awful scare.
I saw it in the reflected light of the street lamp.
Then when Larry and Pip and I looked in later we
saw it sitting by the fire, pretending to wash itself
like cats do. It waved its paw at us.'

Pippin was listening very earnestly indeed.
'This is most interesting,' he said. 'You know—
there doesn't appear to have been any one at all in
the Little Theatre when the robbery was committed
—except the Pantomime Cat! Goon wants to arrest
him. He's sure he doped the manager and robbed
the safe. Would you believe it—the Pantomime
Cat!'

VIII. PIPPIN'S STORY—AND A MEETING

FATTY'S brains began to work at top speed. 'Go on,' he said. 'Tell me all you know. What time were you there, Mr. Pippin—what did you see— how did you discover the robbery and everything ? My goodness, how lucky you were to be on the spot ! '

'Well, actually I was after two rogues I'd seen under a bush the other night,' said Pippin, and Fatty had the grace to blush, though Pippin didn't notice it. 'I thought they might be meeting at the back of the Little Theatre, and I was hiding there. I got there at half-past eight, and when I looked into the room at the back of the verandah—where you saw the Cat—I saw him too. He was lying fast asleep by the fire. Funny to wear a cat-skin so long, isn't it ? '

'Yes. Must be a queer fellow,' said Fatty.

'Well—he *is* queer—queer in the head,' said Pippin. 'I saw him this morning, without his cat-skin. He's not very big, except for his head. He's about twenty-four, they say, but he's never grown up, really. Like a child the way he walks and acts. They call him Boysie.'

'I suppose he got dropped when he was a baby,' said Fatty, remembering stories he had heard. 'Babies like that don't develop properly, do they ? Go on, Mr. Pippin. This is thrilling.'

'Well, I saw the Cat asleep by the fire as I said,' went on Pippin. 'Then, when the clock struck nine I reckoned I'd better hide myself. So I climbed up through a hole in the verandah roof and sat on the window-sill of the room above, waiting. And I heard groans.'

'Go on,' said Fatty, as Pippin paused, remembering. 'Gosh, weren't you lucky to be there!'

'Well, I shone my torch into the room and saw the manager lying stretched out on his desk, and the empty safe in the wall behind him,' said Pippin. 'And I smashed the window and got in. The manager was already coming round. He was doped with some drug. I reckon it had been put into his cup of tea. The safe was quite empty, of course. It's being examined for fingerprints—I got an expert on the job at once—and the cup is being examined for drugs—just a strong sleeping-draught, I expect.'

'Who brought the manager the cup of tea—did he say?' asked Fatty, with interest.

'Yes—the Pantomime Cat!' said Pippin. 'Seems pretty suspicious, doesn't it? But if you talk to Boysie—the Cat—you can't help thinking he'd got nothing to do with the whole thing—he's too silly —he wouldn't have the brains to put a sleeping-draught into a cup of tea, and he certainly wouldn't know where the safe was—or where to get the key —or how to find out the combination of letters that opens the safe door, once the key is in.'

'It's very interesting,' said Fatty. 'Who was in the Little Theatre at the time, besides Boysie?'

'Nobody,' said Pippin. 'Not a soul! All the cast—the actors and actresses, you know—had gone off after the free show they'd given to the children of the Farleigh Homes, and we can check their alibis—find out exactly where they were between

the time of their leaving and eight o'clock. The
deed was done between half-past five and eight—
between the time the show was over and the time
the manager had drunk his cup of tea, and fallen
unconscious.'

'I see. And you've got to check the whereabouts
of all the people who might have gone back and
done the robbery,' said Fatty. 'Yes. But what's to
prevent a stranger doing it—I mean, why should
it be one of the actors?'

'Because whoever did it knew the best time to
do it,' said Pippin. 'He knew where the safe was.
He knew that the manager had put the takings
there the day before and hadn't taken them to the
bank that day as he usually did. He knew where
the key was kept—in the manager's wallet, not on
his key-ring—and he knew that the manager liked
a cup of tea in the evening—and into it went the
sleeping-draught!'

'Yes—you're right. No stranger would have
known all those facts,' said Fatty, thoughtfully.
'It must be one of the cast—either an actor or an
actress. It's queer that Boysie took in the tea,
though, isn't it? Do you think he helped in the
robbery?'

'I don't know! He says he doesn't remember
a thing except feeling very sleepy last night and going
to sleep in front of the fire,' said Pippin. 'That's
certainly where *I* saw him when I looked into the
room. He even says he didn't take in the cup of
tea to the manager, but that's nonsense, of course—
the manager says he certainly did, and he wouldn't
be likely to be mistaken. I think Boysie is scared,
and said he didn't take in the tea to try and clear

himself—forgetting he is quite unmistakable as the Pantomime Cat ! '

' Yes—it looks as if Boysie either did the whole thing or helped somebody else,' said Fatty. ' Well, thanks very much, Pippin. I'll let you know if we spot anything. And remember—don't you give away anything to Goon. He won't thank you for it ! '

' I shan't open my mouth to him,' said Pippin. ' My goodness—here he is, back again—and I haven't even begun this report he wants ! You'd better clear out the back way, Master Frederick.'

Goon loomed up at the front gate, looking most important. He was talking to the vicar, solemnly and ponderously.

Fatty tiptoed out into the hall and made for the kitchen, with Buster in his arms. He meant to go into the back garden, hop over the fence at the bottom and make his way to Pip's. What a lot he had to tell the others !

He heard Goon's loud voice. ' Do you know what the vicar tells me, Pippin ? He tells me you were rude to his brother yesterday—snatched at his hat or something ! Now, I really do think . . .'

But what Goon really did think Fatty didn't wait to hear. Poor Pippin ! He was going to get into trouble over his curiosity about red-headed people now ! Fatty couldn't help feeling very, very sorry !

' If we'd known Pippin was so decent we'd never have thought up all those tricks,' said Fatty to himself, as he made his way to Pip's, where he knew the others would be anxiously awaiting him. ' Still —I can make it up to him, perhaps, by solving this peculiar mystery. The Mystery of the Pantomime Cat. Sounds good ! '

Larry, Daisy, Pip, and Bets had got very impatient indeed, waiting ages for Fatty. He had been gone for an hour and a half! What in the world could he be doing?

' Here he is at last,' called Bets from the window. ' Rushing up the drive with Buster. He looks full of importance—bursting with it. He must have plenty of news! '

He had. He began to relate everything from the very beginning, and when he got to where Goon had actually struck poor Buster with a poker, Bets gave a scream, and flung herself down on the floor beside the surprised Scottie.

' Buster! Are you hurt? Oh, Buster, how *could* any one hit you like that! I hate Goon! I do, I do. I know it's wrong to hate people, but it's wronger *not* to hate cruel people like Goon. Buster, are you bruised? '

The whole tale was hung up for about ten minutes whilst Buster was carefully examined by all the Find-Outers. Fatty had been pretty certain that Buster was not really hurt, for he had an extremely thick coat of hair, but when he saw how concerned the others were, he began to wonder if poor old Buster *had* been badly bruised. The five children tenderly parted the thick hair along Buster's back and examined every speck of the remarkably pink body beneath. Buster was thrilled. He lay down on his tummy, wagging his plumy tail with pleasure at all this loving fuss. In fact he was so thrilled that he hung his red tongue out and began to pant with joy.

There was nothing to be seen at all except for a tiny mark in one place. ' That's where he was hit,' said Bets, triumphantly. ' I wish I could hit *Goon* with a poker—very, very hard.'

' How bloodthirsty you sound, Bets ! ' said Daisy in surprise. ' You know you'd run for miles if Goon so much as yelled at you ! '

' I wouldn't be a bit surprised if Bets *did* take a poker to Goon if she thought he was going to hurt Buster,' said Fatty. ' She may be frightened of him herself—but she'd be all pluck and no fright if she thought he was going to hurt any one else ! I know Bets ! '

Bets was so pleased at this speech from Fatty. She went red and buried her face in Buster's neck. Fatty patted her on the back.

' I felt like banging Goon on the head myself when I twisted the poker out of his hand,' he said. ' Oh my goodness—you should have seen his face when he found that I had the poker and he hadn't ! '

' Go on with the story now,' said Pip. ' It's getting more and more exciting. Gosh, I wish I'd been there.'

Fatty went on with his tale. The children squealed with laughter when they heard that Goon had demanded all the false clues, and had been solemnly handed them by Pippin.

' He'll meet that Sunday train, Fatty ! ' chuckled Pip. ' Can't we meet it too ? '

' Oh *yes*,' begged Bets. ' Let's. Do let's. Goon would be awfully annoyed to see us all there. He'd think we knew the clue too.'

' Which we do,' said Larry. ' Seeing that we thought of it ! '

' Yes—it's an idea,' said Fatty. ' Quite an idea. I've a good mind to disguise myself and arrive on that train—and arouse Goon's Suspicions and get him to follow me.'

'We could all follow too,' giggled Bets. 'We really must do that. It's to-morrow, isn't it. Oh Fatty, wouldn't it be fun ?'

'Go on with the tale,' said Daisy. 'Let's hear it to the end before we make any more plans. It'll be dinner-time before Fatty's finished.'

Fatty then told the rest of the tale to the end. The children were very glad to hear that Pippin had stuck up for Buster and Fatty. They all agreed that Pippin was very nice indeed. They were thrilled to hear about the Pantomime Cat, and the two girls wished they had been brave enough to peep into the verandah-room and see him the night before.

'Do you think he did it all ?' asked Bets. 'If he took in the tea, he must have done it. He may be cleverer than we think.'

'He may be, Bets,' said Fatty. 'I shall have to interview him. In fact, I thought we all could— together, you know, just as if we were children in-terested in him. He may be on his guard with grown-ups. He wouldn't be with children.'

'Yes. That's a good idea,' said Larry. 'Gosh, what a thrill this is ! To think we put our clues in the very place where all this was going to happen— and managed to put a policeman there too, so that he would discover the crime. It's extraordinary.'

'Well—we must set our wits to work,' said Fatty. 'We've only got just over two weeks to solve the mystery—and Goon is on the job too—hampered by a few false clues, of course ! But we've got Pippin to help us. He may learn a few things that it's impossible for us to find out.'

How are we going to set to work ? ' asked Larry.

' We must make a Plan,' said Fatty. ' A properly set-out Plan. Like we usually do. List of Suspects, list of Clues, and so on.'

' Oooh *yes*,' said Bets. ' Let's begin now, Fatty. This very minute. Have you got a note-book ? '

' Of course,' said Fatty, and took out a fat note-book and a very fine fountain-pen. He ruled a few lines very neatly. ' Now then—SUSPECTS.'

A bell sounded loudly from the hall. Bets groaned. ' Blow ! Dinner-time already ! Fatty, will you come this afternoon and do it ? '

' Right,' said Fatty, ' Half-past two every one—and put your best thinking-caps on ! This is the finest mystery we've had yet ! '

IX. PIPPIN IS A HELP

FATTY thought hard during his lunch. His mother found him very silent indeed, and began to wonder about his teeth again. She looked at him closely. His cheeks seemed to have subsided—they were not very swollen now—not more than usual, anyway!

' Frederick—how is your tooth ? ' she asked suddenly.

Fatty looked at his mother blankly. His tooth ? What did she mean ?

' My tooth ? ' he said. ' What tooth, Mother ? '

' Now don't be silly, Frederick,' said his mother. ' You know how swollen your face was this morning. I meant to ring up the dentist but I forgot. I was just asking you how your tooth was—it must have been bad because you had such a swollen face. I think I'd better ring up the dentist, even though your face *has* gone down.'

' Mother,' said Fatty, desperately, ' that wasn't toothache—it was cheek-pads.'

Now it was his mother's turn to look at him blankly. ' Cheek-pads ! What *do* you mean, Frederick ? '

' Things you put in your cheeks to alter your appearance,' explained Fatty, wishing heartily that he had not tried them out on his mother. ' A—a sort of disguise, Mother.'

' How very disgusting,' said his mother. ' I do wish you wouldn't do things like that, Frederick. No wonder you looked so awful.'

' Sorry, Mother,' said Fatty, hoping she would

talk about something else. She did. She talked about the extraordinary behaviour of Mr. Pippin who had snatched at Mr. Twit's hair, or hat, she didn't know which. And she also told Fatty that the vicar had complained about it to Mr. Goon, now that he was back again to take charge of this new robbery case at the Little Theatre.

'And I do hope, Frederick,' said his mother,' I *do* hope you won't try and meddle in *this* case. Apparently Mr. Goon is well on the way to finding out everything, and has a most remarkable collection of clues. I do *not* like that man, but he certainly seems to have been very quick off the mark in this case—came straight back from his holiday, found all these clues, and is on the track of the robber at once !'

' Don't you believe it,' murmured Fatty, half under his breath.

' What did you say, Frederick ? I wish you wouldn't mumble,' said his mother. ' Well, I don't suppose you know a thing about this case, so just keep out of it and don't annoy Mr. Goon.'

Fatty didn't answer. He knew a lot about the case, and he meant to meddle in it for all he was worth, and if he could annoy Mr. Goon he was certainly going to. But he couldn't possibly tell his mother all that ! So he sank into silence once more and began to think hard about all the Suspects.

He would have to find out their names and who they were and where they lived. It was pretty obvious that only one of the theatre people could have committed the crime. One of them had come back that night, let himself in quietly, and done the deed. But which one ?

Fatty decided he must go to Mr. Pippin and get the list of names and addresses. He would do that immediately after his lunch. So, at a quarter to two, when he left the table, Fatty rushed off to see if Mr. Pippin was available. If Goon was at home, it was no good. He couldn't possibly ask Pippin anything in front of Goon.

He walked by the sitting-room window of the little cottage belonging to Goon. Pippin was there, facing the window. Goon was also there, his back to it, writing at the table. Fatty tiptoed to the window and tried to attract Pippin's attention. Pippin looked up, astonished to see Fatty winking and beckoning outside. He turned round cautiously to see what Mr. Goon was doing.

When he turned back again he saw, held up to the window, a piece of paper on which Fatty had written. 'MEET ME IN HIGH STREET TEN MINUTES' TIME.'

Pippin grinned and nodded. Fatty disappeared. Goon heard the click of the gate and turned round.

'Who's that coming in?' said Goon.

'No one,' said Pippin, truthfully.

'Well, who was it going out, then?' said Goon.

'Can't see any one,' said Pippin.

'Gah! Call yourself a policeman and can't see who opens a gate in front of your nose,' said Goon, who had eaten too much lunch and was feeling very bad-tempered. Pippin said nothing at all. He was getting used to Goon's remarks.

He finished what he was doing and then got up. 'Where are you going?' asked Goon.

'Out to the post office,' said Pippin. 'I'm off duty at the moment, Mr. Goon, as you very well know. If there's anything wants doing, I'll do it when I come back.'

And in spite of Goon's snort, Pippin walked out of the house and up to the post office. He posted his letter and then looked for Fatty. Ah, there he was, sitting on the wooden bench. Pippin went up to him. They grinned at one another and Buster rubbed against Pippin's trousers.

'Come into that shop over there and have a lemonade,' said Fatty. 'I don't want Goon to see us hob-nobbing together.'

They went into the little shop, sat down, and Fatty ordered lemonades. Then, in a low voice, Fatty told Pippin what he wanted.

'Do you know the names and addresses of the actors and actresses at the Little Theatre?' he asked.

'Yes,' said Pippin, at once. 'I got them all last night. Wait a bit—I think they're in my note-book. I don't believe I gave them to Mr. Goon. He's been out interviewing the whole lot, and I expect he got the names from the manager—same as I did.'

'Oh—he's interviewed them already, has he?' said Fatty. 'He can get going when he likes, can't he?'

'Yes,' said Pippin. 'He's found one of them has a name beginning with Z too—you know one of the clues was an old handkerchief with Z on it. Well, see here,' and he pointed to one of the names in the list he was now showing to Fatty, 'the name of Dick Whittington, the principal boy—who's acted by a girl—is Zoe Markham. Looks as if Zoe was out on that verandah for some reason or other—at a meeting of the crooks, perhaps.'

Fatty was horror-stricken. To think that there was actually somebody with a name beginning with Z! Who would have thought it? He didn't know what to say. At all costs he would have to clear Zoe somehow. Fatty wished very heartily for the hundredth time that he and the others hadn't started Pippin on a false mystery complete with false clues.

'Has Zoe got an alibi—some one to swear that she was somewhere else between half-past five and eight o'clock?' asked Fatty, looking worried.

'Oh yes. They've all got alibis,' said Pippin. 'Every one of them. I interviewed them myself last night, the whole lot—and Mr. Goon gave them the once-over again this morning. Alibis all correct.'

'Queer, isn't it,' said Fatty, after a silence. 'I mean—it *must* be one of those theatre people, mustn't it? Nobody else had so much inside knowledge as to be able to give the manager a cup of tea, and then take down the mirror, find the key, work out the combination, and open the safe.'

'Don't forget it was the Pantomime Cat who took in the cup of tea,' said Pippin.

'Yes. That's queerer still,' said Fatty. 'Any one would think he'd done the job.'

'Goon thinks so,' said Pippin. 'He thinks all that business of the Cat saying he doesn't understand, and he doesn't remember, and bursting into tears is put on—good acting, you know.'

'What do *you* think?' asked Fatty. Pippin considered. 'I told you before. I think Boysie's a bit queer in the head—never grown up, poor fellow. You know, I've got a cousin like that—and he

wouldn't hurt a fly. It's a fact, he wouldn't. I
don't see how he could possibly have done all that.
I'm sorry Mr. Goon's got it into his head that
Boysie's done the job—he'll scare the poor chap
into fits.'

'Well—it's quite possible that somebody hid in
the kitchen somewhere when Boysie was making
the tea, and popped something into the cup when
Boysie wasn't looking,' said Fatty.

'Yes. There's something in that,' said Pippin.
'But we still come back to the fact that it can only
have been done by one of the theatre folk—no one
else knows enough to have done it—and they all
have alibis—so there you are!'

'Can I have their names and addresses?' asked
Fatty. 'I'll copy them down.' Pippin handed him
over his note-book. Fatty looked through the
pages with interest. 'I say—are these your notes
about where they said they were between half-past
five and eight o'clock last night?'

'That's right,' said Pippin. 'Take them along
with you, if you like. Save you a lot of trouble!
They've all been interviewed twice, so you can take
my word for it they won't say anything different the
third time—that's if you were thinking of interviewing them, Master Frederick.'

'We're making out a Plan,' said Fatty, stuffing
the notes into his pocket. 'I don't quite know what
it will be yet. I'll tell you when we know details.
Thanks most awfully, Mr. Pippin.'

'If you ever see a villainous-looking tramp with
red hair, let me know, will you?' said Pippin. 'I
mean—you get about a lot on that bike of yours
—and you might happen on the fellow—and his

6

mate with him. The ones I saw under the bush that night in Willow Road, I mean.'

'Er—yes—I know the ones you mean,' said Fatty, feeling extremely guilty, at this mention of the red-haired villain. 'I'll certainly let you know if I see him again. But I don't think he had anything to do with this robbery job, you know.'

'Ah, you can't tell,' said Pippin, finishing his glass of lemonade and standing up. 'If ever I saw wickedness in any one's face it was in that red-haired fellow's. I wouldn't care to be seen in *his* company. I'll walk a little way with you, Master Frederick—it's a nice day. Your dog all right now?'

'Quite, thanks,' said Fatty. 'Takes a lot to bruise a Scottie with as thick a coat as Buster!'

'That properly turned me against Mr. Goon, that did,' said Pippin, as they walked down the High Street—and round the corner they bumped straight into Mr. Goon! He glared at them both, and Buster flew round him delightedly.

'Buster, come here,' ordered Fatty, in such a stern voice that Buster felt he had to obey. He put his tail down and crept behind Fatty, keeping up a continuous growl.

'You be careful of the company you keep, Pippin,' ordered Mr. Goon. 'I warned you against that boy, didn't I? Always interfering and meddling, he is! Anyway, he can't interfere in *this* Case much! Cast-iron, that's what it is! I'll be making an arrest any time now!'

Mr. Goon walked on, and Pippin and Fatty looked at one another with raised eyebrows.

'It's that Pantomime Cat he's going to arrest,' said Pippin. 'I saw it in his eyes! And before he's

finished with that poor Cat he'll make him confess
to things he didn't do.   He will ! '

'Then I'll have to see that he doesn't,' said
Fatty.   'I must set the old brains to work
IMMEDIATELY ! '

X. THE SUSPECTS AND THEIR ALIBIS

AT just after half-past two Fatty walked into Pip's drive for the second time that day, and was hailed by Bets from the open window.

'Hurry up, Fatty! We want to make our Plan!'

Fatty hurried, grinning at Bets' impatience. He went up the stairs two at a time, and found the other four waiting for him round the table.

'Ha! A Conference!' said Fatty. 'Well—I've got some information here which we'll study together. Then we'll really get going.'

He told the children quickly what Pippin had told him, and then got out the note-book with names, addresses and particulars of alibis in. The word 'alibi' was new to Bets, and had to be explained to her.

'Is it anything to do with lullaby?' she asked, and the others roared.

'No, Bets,' said Fatty. 'I'll tell you what an alibi is. Suppose somebody smashed this window, and your mother thought it was Pip—and Pip told her he was with me at the time, and I said yes, he certainly was—then I am Pip's *alibi*—he's got his alibi, because I can vouch for his being with me when the window was smashed.'

'I see,' said Bets. 'And if somebody said that at just this moment you had hit Goon on the head, and we said no, you couldn't have, because you were with us—we'd *all* be alibis for you.'

'Quite right, Bets—you've got the idea,' grinned

76

Fatty. ' Well—I've got a list of the alibis of all the Suspects here—which will be very, very useful. Listen, and I'll read out the names of the Suspects first, and then I'll tell you their alibis and what we know about them.'

He read from Pippin's notes.

SUSPECTS

No. 1. *Pantomime Cat*, otherwise Boysie Summers. Was in theatre at the time in question. Took Manager in a cup of tea before eight o'clock. Says he didn't, but admits he had a cup of tea himself. Says he went to sleep most of evening.

No. 2. *Zoe Markham*, who takes part of Dick Whittington. Says she left theatre with other members of the cast, and went to her sister's, where she played with the children and helped to put them to bed. Her sister is Mrs. Thomas, and lives at Green House, Hemal Road.

' I know her ! ' said Daisy. ' She's awfully nice. She's got two dear little children. One's having a birthday soon, I know.'

' I say,' said Larry, suddenly, ' *Zoe* Markham ! I hope Goon doesn't connect up the Z for Zoe with the Z on that old hanky of Daisy's—the one we used for a false clue.'

' I rather think he has,' said Fatty. ' We'll have to do something about that, if so. Well—to continue . . ."

No. 3. *Lucy White*, who takes the part of Margot, Dick Whittington's sweetheart. Says she went to call on Miss Adams, an old-age pensioner who is ill, address 11 Mark Street. Sat with her till nine o'clock, and helped her with her knitting.

' Miss Adams is a friend of our cook's,' said Larry. ' She used to come and help with the sewing. Nice old thing she was.'

No. 4. Peter Watting, who takes the part of Dick's master,' went on Fatty. ' Elderly, and rather obstructive. Would not answer questions readily. Said he was out walking with Suspect No. 5 at the time.

Suspect No. 5. William Orr, who takes the part of the captain of Dick's ship. Young man, affable and helpful. Says he was out walking with Peter Watting at the time.

' Then those two are alibis for each other,' said Larry, with interest. ' What's to stop them from *both* going back to the theatre and doing the robbery, and then giving each other an alibi ? '

' That's a good point, Larry,' said Fatty. ' Very good point. Pippin doesn't seem to have worked that out. Wait a bit—here's another note about it. " Suspects 4 and 5 (Peter Watting and William Orr) further said they had gone for a walk by the river, and had called at a tea-house called ' The Turret ' for some sandwiches and coffee. They did not know the exact time ".'

' Bit fishy, I think,' said Pip. ' Wants looking into.'

'I'VE GOT A LIST OF THE ALIBIS OF ALL THE SUSPECTS HERE—
WHICH WILL BE VERY USEFUL.'

Suspect No. 6. *Alec Grant*, who takes the part of Dick's mother. Usually takes women's parts and is very good at them, a fine mimic and good actor. Says he was giving a show at Hetton Hall, Sheepridge, that evening, from six to ten—acting various women's parts to an audience of about one hundred.

'Well! That rules *him* out!' said Larry. 'He's got a hundred alibis, not one.'

'Yes. It certainly clears *him*,' said Fatty. 'Well, here's the last Suspect.'

Suspect No. 7. *John James*, who plays the part of the black king in the play. Says he went to the cinema and was there all the evening, seeing the film called 'You know How it is.'

'Not much of an alibi either,' said Pip. 'He could easily have popped in, and popped out again—and even popped back again after doing the robbery. Poor alibi, I call that.'

'Well now,' said Fatty, 'I imagine that Goon will check all these, if he hasn't already—but he's such a mutt that I expect he'll miss something important that *we* might spot. So I vote we all check up on the various alibis ourselves.'

There was a deep silence. Nobody felt capable of doing this. It was bad enough to interview people—it was much worse to check an alibi!

'I can't,' said Bets, at last. 'I know I'm a Find-Outer and I ought to do what you tell me, Fatty, but I really *can't* check an ali—alibi. I mean —it sounds too much like a *real* detective.'

'Well, we may be kids, but we're jolly good detectives all the same,' said Fatty. 'Look at all the mysteries we've solved already! This is a bit more *advanced*, perhaps.'

'It's frightfully advanced,' groaned Larry. 'I feel rather like Bets—out of my depth.'

'Don't give up before you've begun,' said Fatty. 'Now, I'll tell you what I propose we do.'

'What?' asked every one, and Buster thumped his tail on the ground as if he too had a great interest in the question.

'There are three things we must do,' said Fatty. 'We must interview Boysie, and see what *we* think of him—and we'll interview him all together, as we suggested before.'

'Right,' said Larry. 'What next?'

'We'll see every other suspect too,' said Fatty. There was a general groan.

'Oh *no*, Fatty—six people! And all grown-up! We can't possibly,' said Daisy. 'What excuse would we have for seeing them, even?'

'A very good excuse indeed,' said Fatty. 'All we've got to do is to find our autograph-books and go and ask for autographs—and we can easily say a few words to them then, can't we?'

'That's a *brilliant* idea,' said Pip. 'Really brilliant, Fatty. I must say you think of good ideas.'

'Oh well,' said Fatty, modestly, 'I've got a few brains, you know. As a matter of fact . . .'

'*Don't* start telling us about the wonderful things you did at school last term,' begged Pip. 'Go on with our Plan.'

'All right,' said Fatty, a little huffily. 'The third thing we must do, is, as I said, check up on the alibis—and if we think hard, it won't be so fright-fully difficult. For instance, Daisy says she knows Zoe Markham's sister, who lives near her, and she also says one of the children is having a birthday soon. Well, Daisy, what's to stop you and Bets from taking the child a present, getting into con-versation with the mother, and finding out if Zoe *was* there all that evening? Zoe's sister wouldn't be on her guard with two children who came with a present for her child.'

' Yes—all right, Fatty, I can do that,' said Daisy. ' You'll come too, won't you, Bets? '

' Yes,' said Bets. ' But you'll ask the questions, won't you, Daisy? '

' You've got to help,' said Daisy. ' I'm not doing it all! '

' Now the next Suspect is Lucy White who went to sit with Miss Adams, an old-age pensioner,' went on Fatty. ' Larry, you said she was a friend of your cook's, and used to come to help with the sewing. Can't you and Daisy concoct some sort of sewing job you want done, and take it round to her—and put a few questions about Lucy White? '

' Yes, we could,' said Daisy. ' I'll pretend I want to give Mother a surprise for Easter, and I'll take round a cushion-cover I want embroidering, or something. I've been there before, and Mary Adams knows me.'

' Splendid,' said Fatty. ' That's two alibis we can check very easily indeed. Now the next one—well, the next two, actually, because they are each other's alibis—Peter Watting and William Orr. Well, they apparently went to a place called The Turret and had coffee and sandwiches there. Pip,

you and I will call there and also have coffee and
sandwiches to-morrow morning.'

'But it's Sunday and I have to go to church,'
objected Pip.

'Oh yes. I forgot it was Sunday,' said Fatty.
'Well, we'll do that on Monday or Tuesday morning.
Now, Suspect No. 6 is Alec Grant, who was
apparently giving a concert at Hetton Hall to about
a hundred people. Seems hardly necessary to check
that.'

'Well, don't let's,' said Larry.

'The thing is—a really good detective always
checks *every*thing,' said Fatty. 'Even if he thinks it
really isn't necessary. So I suppose we'd better
check that too. Bets, you can come with me and
check it. We'll find some one who attended the
show, and ask them about it and see if Alec Grant
really was there.'

'Right,' said Bets, who never minded what
she did with Fatty. She always felt so safe with
him, as safe as if she was with a grown-up.

'That only leaves one more,' said Fatty, looking
at his list. 'And that's John James who says he went
to the cinema all the evening.'

'Yes—and we thought it was a pretty poor alibi,'
said Pip. 'Who's going to check that one up?'

'Oh—Larry and I could tackle that, I think,
or you and Larry,' said Fatty.

'But how?' asked Larry.

'Have to think of something,' said Fatty. 'Well,
there you are, Find-Outers—plenty for us to find
out! We've got to see Boysie, got to get autographs
from all the cast, and have a look at them—and got
to check up all the alibis. Pretty stiff work.'

' *And*, Fatty, we've got to meet that train to-morrow and lead old Goon a dance,' Bets reminded him. ' Don't let's forget that ! '

' Oh no—we really must do that,' grinned Fatty. ' I'll use my new cheek-pads for that.'

' Whatever are those ? ' said Bets in wonder, and screamed with laughter when Fatty told her. ' Oh yes, do wear those. I hope I don't giggle when I see you.'

' You'd better not, young Bets,' said Fatty, getting hold of her nose and pulling it gently. ' Now what time's that train we underlined ? '

' Half-past three to-morrow afternoon,' said Pip. ' We'll all be there, Fatty. What will *you* do—go to the next station, catch the train there, and arrive here at 3.30 ? '

' I will,' said Fatty. ' Look out for me. So long, every one. I've just remembered that my mother told me to be home an hour ago, to meet my great-aunt. *What* a memory I've got ! '

XI. TREAT FOR MR. GOON

FATTY worked out the time-table for putting the Plan into action, that evening. They couldn't do much the next day, Sunday, that was certain. Daisy had better buy a present for Zoe's sister's child on Monday and take it in with Bets. The next day perhaps she and Larry could go and see Miss Adams and find out about Lucy White.

He and Larry would go to The Turret on Monday and have coffee and sandwiches and see if they could find out anything about Peter Watting and William Orr. They could leave Alec Grant till last, because it really did seem as if his alibi was unshakable, as it consisted of about a hundred people. He would not dare to give an alibi like that if it were not true.

' I can't think how to find out about the last fellow's alibi—what's his name—John James,' said Fatty to himself. ' Can't very well go and talk to a cinema and ask it questions ! Still, I'll think of something.'

He paused and looked at himself in the mirror. He was thinking out his disguise for the next day —something perfectly reasonable, but peculiar, and with red hair so that it would attract Goon's attention. He would wear dark glasses and pretend to be short-sighted. That would make the children want to laugh.

' We'll go and see Boysie—what a name—on Monday morning,' thought Fatty, drawing a line

round both his nostrils to see what effect it gave.
' Gracious ! Don't I look bad-tempered ! Grrrrr !
Gah ! '

He removed the lines and experimented with
different eyebrows, thinking of his Plan all the
time.

' We'll all go and ask for autographs after the
afternoon performance at the Little Theatre on
Monday,' thought Fatty. 'And dear me—why
shouldn't we *go* to the performance and see every one
in action. It mightn't tell us anything—but on the
other hand, it might ! That's a jolly good idea.
Well—Monday's going to be pretty busy, I can see,
what with interviewing and asking for autographs
and checking up alibis. Now, what about that
train to-morrow ? Shall I speak to Goon when I
see him or not ? I'll ask him the way somewhere ! '

He began to practise different voices. First,
a deep-down rumble, modelled on a preacher who
had come to his school to preach one Sunday, and
who had been the admiration of every one because of
his extremely bass voice.

He tried a high falsetto voice—no, not so good.
He tried a foreign voice—ah, that was splendid.

' Please, Sair, to tell me ze way to Hoffle-Foffle
Road ! ' began Fatty. 'What you say, Sair ? I
not unnerstand. I say, I weesh to know ze way
to Hoffle-Foffle Road. HOFFLE-FOFFLE ! '

There came a knock at his door. ' Frederick.
Have you got Pip and the others in there with you ?
You know I don't like them here so late at night.'

Fatty opened his door in surprise. ' Oh no,
Mother—of course they're not here. There's only
me ! '

His mother looked at him and made an exasperated noise. 'Frederick! What have you done to your eyebrows, they are all crooked! And what's that round your eye?'

'Oh—only a wrinkle I drew there for an experiment,' said Fatty, rubbing it away hastily. 'And you needn't worry about my eyebrows, Mother. They're not really crooked. Look.'

He took off the eyebrows he was wearing, and showed his mother his own underneath. They were not at all crooked, of course!

'Well, what will you think of next, Frederick?' said his mother, half-crossly. 'I came to say that your father wants you to listen to the next bit on the wireless with him—it's about a part of China he knows very well. Are you *sure* you haven't got any one else with you here? I did hear quite a lot of voices when I was coming up the stairs.'

'Mother, look under the bed, behind the curtains and in the cupboard,' said Fatty, generously. But she wouldn't, of course, and proceeded downstairs —to stop in a hurry when she heard a falsetto voice say, 'Has she gone? Can I come out?'

She turned at once, annoyed to think there was some one in Fatty's room after all—but when she saw Fatty's grinning face, she laughed too.

'Oh—one of your Voices, I suppose,' she said. 'I might have guessed. I cannot think, Frederick, how it is that you always have such good reports from school. I cannot believe you behave well there.'

'Well, Mother,' said Fatty, in his most modest voice, 'the fact is, brains *will* tell, you know. I can't help having good brains, can I? I mean . . .'

' Sh ! ' said his father, as they walked into the sitting-room. ' The talk's begun.'

So it had—and a very dull talk it proved to be, on a little-known part of China, which Fatty devoutly hoped he would never have to visit. He passed the dull half-hour by thinking out further plans. His father was really pleased to see such an intent look on Fatty's face.

The Find-Outers were finding the time very long, as they always did when something exciting was due to happen. Bets could hardly wait for the next afternoon to come. How would Fatty be disguised ? What would he say ? Would he wink at them ?

At twenty-five past three Larry, Daisy, Pip, and Bets walked sedately on to the platform. A minute later Goon arrived, a little out of breath, because he had had an argument with P.C. Pippin, and had had to hurry. He saw the children at once and glared at them.

' What you here for ? ' he demanded.

' Same reason as you, I suppose,' said Pip. ' To meet some one.'

' We're meeting Fatty,' piped up Bets, and got a nudge from Larry.

' It's all right,' whispered Bets. ' I'm not giving anything away, really—he won't know it's Fatty when he sees him—you know he won't.'

The train came in with a clatter and stopped. Quite a lot of people got out. Mr. Goon eyed them all carefully. He was standing by the platform door, leading to the booking-office, and every one had to pass him to give up their tickets. The four children stood near by, watching out for Fatty.

Bets nudged Pip. A voluminous old lady was proceeding down the platform, a veil spreading out behind her in the wind. Pip shook his head. No —good as Fatty was at disguises he could never look like that imperious old lady.

A man came by, hobbling along with a stick, his hat pulled down over his eyes, and a shapeless mackintosh flung across his shoulders. He had a straggling moustache and an absurd little beard. His hair was a little reddish, and Goon gave him a very sharp look indeed.

But Bets knew it wasn't Fatty. This man had a crooked nose, and Fatty surely couldn't mimic a thing like that.

It looked almost as if Goon was about to follow this man—and then he saw some one else —some one with *much* redder hair, some one *much* more suspicious.

This man was evidently a foreigner of some sort. He wore a peculiar hat on his red hair, which was neatly brushed. He had a foreign-looking cape round his shoulders, and brightly polished, pointed shoes.

For some peculiar reason he wore bicycle-clips round the bottoms of his trousers, and this made him even more foreign-looking, though Bets didn't quite know why it should. The man wore dark glasses on his nose, had a little red moustache, and his cheeks were very bulgy. He was very freckled indeed. Bets wondered admiringly how Fatty managed to produce freckles like that.

She knew it was Fatty, of course, and so did the others, though if they had not been actually looking for him, they would have been very doubtful indeed.

7

But there was something about the jaunty way he walked and looked about that made them quite certain.

The foreigner brushed against Bets as he came to the exit. He dug his elbow into her, and she almost giggled.

'Your ticket, sir,' said the collector, as Fatty seemed to have forgotten all about this. Fatty began to feel in all his pockets, one after another, exclaiming in annoyance.

'This tick-ett! I had him, I know I had him! He was green.'

Mr. Goon watched him intently, quite ready to arrest him if he didn't produce his ticket! The foreigner suddenly swooped down by Goon's feet, and shoved one of them aside with his hand. Goon glared.

'Here. What are you doing?' he began.

'A million apologeeeze,' said the stranger, waving his ticket in Goon's face, and almost scraping the skin off the end of the policeman's big nose. 'I have him—he was on the ground, and you put your beeg foots on him. Aha!'

Fatty thrust the ticket at the astonished collector, and pushed past Goon. Then he stopped so suddenly that Goon jumped.

'Ah, you are the pliss, are you not?' demanded Fatty, peering at Goon short-sightedly from his dark glasses. 'At first I think you are an engine-driver—but now I see you are the pliss.'

'Yes. I'm the police,' said Mr. Goon, gruffly, feeling more and more suspicious of this behaviour. 'Where do you want to go? I expect you're a stranger here.'

'Ah yes, alas! A strangair,' agreed Fatty. 'I need to know my way to a place. You will tell me zis place?'

'Certainly,' said Goon, only too pleased.

'It is—er—it is—Hoffle-Foffle House, in Willow Road,' said Fatty, making a great to-do with the Hoffle-Foffle bit. Goon looked blank.

'No such place as—er—what you said,' he answered.

'I say Hoffle-Foffle—you say you do not know it? How can zis be?' cried Fatty, and walked out into the road at top speed, with Goon at his heels. Fatty stopped abruptly and Goon bumped into him. Bets by this time was so convulsed with laughter that she had to stay behind.

'There *isn't* a house of that name,' said Goon, exasperated. 'Who do you want to see?'

'That ees my own beeziness—vairy, vairy secret beeziness,' said Fatty. 'Where is zis Willow Road? I will find Hoffle-Foffle by myself.'

Goon directed him. Fatty set off at top speed again, and Goon followed, panting. The four children followed too, trying to suppress their giggles. Hoffle-Foffle House was, of course, not to be found.

'I will sairch the town till I see zis place,' Fatty told Mr. Goon, earnestly. 'Do not accompany me, Mr. Pliss—I am tired of you.'

Whereupon Fatty set off at a great pace again, and left Mr. Goon behind. He saw the four children still following, and frowned. Little pests! Couldn't he shadow any one without them coming too? 'Clear-orf!' he said to them, as they came up. 'Do you hear me? Clear-orf!'

'Can't we even go for a walk, Mr. Goon?' said Daisy, pathetically, and Mr. Goon snorted and hastened to follow 'that dratted foreigner,' who by now was almost out of sight.

Mr. Goon, in fact, almost lost him. Fatty was getting tired of this protracted walk, and wanted to throw Mr. Goon off, and go home and laugh with the others. But Mr. Goon valiantly pursued him. So Fatty made a pretence of examining the names of many houses, peering at them through his dark glasses. He was getting nearer and nearer to his own home by this time.

He managed to pop in at his front gate and scuttled down to the shed at the bottom of the garden, where he locked the door, and began to pull off his disguise as quickly as he could. He wiped his face free of paint, pulled off his false eyebrows and wig, took out his cheek-pads, straightened his tie, and ventured out into the garden.

He saw the four children looking anxiously over the fence. 'Goon's gone in to tell your mother,' whispered Larry. 'He thinks the suspicious foreigner is somewhere in the garden and he wants permission to search for him.'

'Let him,' grinned Fatty. 'Oh my, how I want to laugh! Sh! Here's Goon and Mother.'

Fatty strolled up to meet them. 'Why, Mr. Goon,' he began, 'what a pleasant surprise!'

'I thought those friends of yours had gone to meet you at the station,' said Mr. Goon, suspiciously.

'Quite right,' said Fatty, politely. 'They did meet me. Here they are.'

The other four had gone in at the gate at the

bottom of the garden, and were now trooping demurely up the garden path behind Fatty. Goon stared at them in surprise.

'But—they've been following *me* about all the afternoon,' he began.' 'And I certainly didn't see you at the station.'

'Oh but, Mr. Goon, he *was* there,' said Larry, earnestly. 'Perhaps you didn't recognize him. He does look different sometimes, you know.'

'Mr. Goon,' interrupted Mrs. Trotteville, impatiently, 'you wanted to look for some suspicious trespasser in my garden. It's Sunday afternoon and I want to go back to my husband. Never mind about these children.'

'Yes, but,' began Mr. Goon, trying to sort things out in his mind, and failing. How *could* these kids have met Fatty if he wasn't there? How dared they say they had met him, when he knew jolly well the four of them had been trailing him all that afternoon? There was something very peculiar here.

'Well, Mr. Goon, I'll leave you,' said Mrs. Trotteville. 'I've no doubt the children will help you to look for your suspicious loiterer.'

She went in. The children began to look everywhere with such terrific enthusiasm that Mr. Goon gave it up. He was sure he'd never find that red-haired foreigner again. *Could* it have been Fatty in one of his disguises? No—not possibly! Nobody would have the sauce to lead him on a wild-goose-chase like that. And now he hadn't solved the mystery of who was coming by that 3.30 train! He snorted and went crossly out of the front gate.

The children flung themselves down on the

damp ground and laughed till they cried. They laughed so much that they didn't see a very puzzled Mr. Goon looking over the fence at them. *Now* what was the joke? Those dratted children! Slippery as eels they were—couldn't trust them an inch!

Mr. Goon went back home, tired and cross. ' Interfering with the Law! ' he muttered, to P.C. Pippin's surprise. ' Always interfering with the Law! One of these days I'll catch them good and proper—and then they'll laugh the other side of their faces. Gah! '

XII. ZOE, THE FIRST SUSPECT

THE next day, Monday, the Five Find-Outers really set to work. They all met at Pip's as usual. They were early, half-past nine—but, as Fatty pointed out, they had a lot to do.

'You and Bets must go and buy a birthday present for that child—Zoe Markham's niece,' he said. 'Got any money?'

'I haven't any at all,' said Bets. 'I owed Pip three and threepence for a water-pistol, and it's all gone to pay for that.'

'I've got about a shilling, I think,' said Daisy.

Fatty put his hand into his pocket and pulled out some silver. He always seemed to have plenty of money. He had aunts and uncles who tipped him well, and he was just like a grown-up the way he always seemed to have enough to spend.

He picked out a two shilling piece and a sixpence. 'Here you are, Daisy. You can get a little something for half-a-crown. When's the child's birthday?'

'To-morrow,' said Daisy, 'I met her little sister yesterday and asked her.'

'Good,' said Fatty. 'Couldn't be better! Now you go and buy something, you and Bets, and put a message on it, and deliver it to Mrs. Thomas, Zoe's sister. And mind you get into conversation with her and find out exactly when Zoe went there on Friday night, and what time she left.'

'How shall we get her talking, though?' said Daisy, beginning to feel nervous.

Fatty looked sternly at poor Daisy. 'Now I really can't plan every one's conversation! It's up to you to get this done, Daisy. Use your common-sense. Ask what the mother herself is giving the child—something like that—and I bet she'll take you in to see the present she's prepared.'

'Oh yes—that's a good idea,' said Daisy, cheering up. 'Come on, Bets—we'll go and do our bit of shopping.'

'I'm going to see Pippin for a few minutes, if I can,' said Fatty. 'I want to find out one or two things before I make further plans.'

'What do you want to know?' asked Larry, interested.

'Well—I want to know if there were any finger-prints on that wall-mirror, which had to be lifted down to get the safe open, at the back of it,' said Fatty. 'And there might have been prints on the safe too. If there were, and the job was done by one of the actors or actresses, we might as well give up our detecting at once—because Goon has only got to take every one's fingerprints, compare them with the ones on mirror or safe—and there you are. He'd have the thief immediately!'

'Oh, I hope he won't!' said Bets, in dismay. 'I want to go on with this mystery. I want *us* to solve it, not Goon. I like this finding-out part.'

'Don't worry,' said Fatty, with a grin. 'The thief wouldn't leave prints behind, I'm sure! He was pretty cunning, whoever he was.'

'Do you think it *was* Boysie, the Pantomime Cat?' asked Daisy.

'No—not at present, anyway,' said Fatty. 'Wait and see what we think of him when we see him. Oh, and Larry, will you and Pip go along to the theatre this morning and get tickets for this afternoon's show? Here's the money.'

And out came the handful of silver again!

'It's a good thing you're so *rich*, Fatty,' said Bets. 'We wouldn't find detecting nearly so easy if you weren't!'

'Now, let's see,' said Fatty. 'We've all got jobs to do this morning, haven't we? Report back here at twelve, or as near that as possible. I'm off to see Pippin, if I can manage to get him alone. Come on, Buster. Wake up! Bicycle basket for you!'

Buster opened his eyes, got up from the hearth-rug, yawned and wagged his tail. He trotted sedately after Fatty. Bets went to put on her hat and coat, ready to do the bit of birthday shopping with Daisy. Pip and Larry went to get their bicycles, meaning to ride down to the Little Theatre to get the tickets.

Fatty was just wheeling his bicycle from Pip's shed. He called to the other two. 'Pip! Larry! Don't just buy the tickets—talk to as many people down there as you can! See if you can find out anything at all.'

'Right, Captain!' grinned Larry. 'We'll do our best.'

Off went all the Five Find-Outers—and Dog—to do a really good morning's work of Detection. Bets and Daisy walked, as Bets' bike had a puncture. They were soon down in the town, and went to the toy-shop there.

'Jane's only four,' said Daisy. 'She won't want anything too advanced. It's no good buying her a game or a jigsaw. We'll look at the soft toys.'

But there was no soft toy for half-a-crown—

they were all much too expensive. Then Bets pounced on a set of dolls' furniture, for a doll's house.

' Oh, look ! Isn't it sweet ! Let's get this, Daisy. Two tiny chairs, a table and a sofa—lovely ! I'm sure Jane would love it.'

' How much is it ? ' said Daisy, looking at the price-label. ' Two shillings and ninepence ha'penny. Well, I've got Fatty's half-crown, and I'll put the other threepence ha'penny to it myself.'

' I'll give you the next penny I get,' said Bets. ' Oh, I do like these little chairs ! '

Daisy bought the doll's furniture, and had it wrapped up nicely. ' Now we'll go home and write a message on a label, and take it to Jane's mother,' said Daisy. So off they went, and wrote the label. ' Many happy returns to Jane, with love from Daisy and Bets.'

Then they set off once more to call on Mrs. Thomas, Zoe's sister. They came to the house, a small pretty one, set back from the road. They stopped at the gate.

Daisy was nervous. ' Now, whatever shall we do if Mrs. Thomas isn't in ? '

' Say we'll come again,' said Bets, promptly. ' But she will be in. I can hear Jane and Dora playing in the garden.'

' What shall we say when the door is opened ? ' asked Daisy, still nervous.

' Just say we've got a present for little Jane, and then see what Mrs. Thomas says,' said Bets, surprised to see how nervous Daisy was. ' *I'll* manage this if you can't, Daisy.'

That was quite enough to make Daisy forget

all her nervousness! 'I can manage it all right, thank you,' she said, huffily. 'Come on!'

They went to the front door and rang the bell. Mrs. Thomas opened the door. 'Hallo, Daisy!' she said. 'And who is this—oh, little Elizabeth Hilton, isn't it?'

'Yes,' said Bets, whose name really was Elizabeth.

'Er—it's Jane's birthday to-morrow, isn't it.' began Daisy. 'We've brought her a little present, Mrs. Thomas.'

'How kind of you!' said Mrs. Thomas. 'What is it?'

Daisy gave it to her. 'It's just some dolls' furniture,' she said. 'Has she got a doll's house?'

'Well, isn't that strange—her daddy and I are giving Jane a doll's house to-morrow!' said Mrs. Thomas. 'This furniture will be *just* right!'

'Oh—*could* we see the doll's house, please?' asked Bets at once, seeing a wonderful chance of getting into the house and talking.

'Of course,' said Mrs. Thomas. 'Come in.'

So in they went and were soon being shown a lovely little doll's house in an upstairs room. Daisy led the talk round to the Little Theatre.

'Your sister Zoe Summers plays in the shows at the Little Theatre, doesn't she?' she said, innocently.

'Yes,' said Mrs. Thomas. 'Have you seen any of the shows?'

'We're going this afternoon,' said Bets. 'I do want to see that Pantomime Cat.'

'Poor Cat!' said Mrs. Thomas. 'Poor Boysie. He's in a dreadful state now—that awful policeman has been at him, you know—he thinks Boysie did that robbery. I expect you heard about it.'

Just as she said that a tall and pretty young woman came into the room. ' Hallo ! ' she said. ' I thought I heard voices up here. Who are these friends of yours, Helen ? '

' This is Daisy and this is Elizabeth, or Bets—that's what you are called, isn't it ? ' said Mrs. Thomas, turning to Bets. ' This is Zoe—my sister—the one who plays in the shows at the Little Theatre.

Well ! *What* a bit of luck ! Daisy and Bets stared earnestly at Zoe. How pretty she was—and what a smiley face. They liked her very much.

' Did I hear you talking about poor Boysie ? ' said Zoe, sitting down by the doll's house, and beginning to rearrange the furniture in it. ' It's a shame ! As if he could have done that job on Friday evening ! He hasn't got the brains—he'd never, never think of it, even to get back on the manager for his unkindness.'

' Why—is the manager unkind to Boysie ? ' asked Bets.

' Yes—awfully impatient with him. You see,' said Zoe, ' Boysie is slow, and he's only given silly parts like Dick Whittington's Cat or Mother Goose's Goose and things like that—and the manager shouts at him till poor old Boysie gets worse than ever. I couldn't bear it on Friday morning, when we had a rehearsal—I flared up and told the manager what I thought of him ! '

' Did you really ? ' said Daisy. ' Was he angry ? '

' Yes, very,' said Zoe. ' We had a real shouting match, and he told me I could leave at the end of this week.'

' Oh dear,' said Daisy. ' So you've lost your job, then ? '

' Yes. But I don't mind. I'm tired and I want a rest,' said Zoe. ' I'm coming to stay with my sister here for a bit. We shall both like that.'

' I expect you thought it served the manager right, when he was drugged and robbed that night,' said Daisy. ' Where were you when it happened ? '

' I left at half-past five with the others,' said Zoe. ' And came here. I believe old Goon thinks I did the robbery, with Boysie to help me ! '

' But how could he, if you were here all the evening ? ' said Bets at once. ' Didn't your sister tell Mr. Goon you were here ? '

' Yes—but unfortunately I went out at a quarter to seven, after I'd put the children to bed, to go to the post office,' said Zoe. ' And my sister didn't hear me come back ten minutes later ! I went up to my bedroom and stayed there till about a quarter to eight and then came down again. So, you see, according to Mr. Goon, I could have slipped down to the Little Theatre, put a sleeping-draught into the manager's cup of tea, taken down the mirror, opened the safe and stolen the money—all with poor Boysie's help ! *And* Goon has actually found a handkerchief—it isn't mine, by the way—with Z on, on the verandah at the back of the Theatre—and he says I dropped it when Boysie let me in that night. What do you think of *that* ? '

XIII. LARRY AND PIP ON THE JOB

THE two girls were full of horror—especially at the mention of that unfortunate handkerchief. Daisy went scarlet when she remembered how she had sewn a Z on it in one corner, never, never thinking that there might be any one called Zoe.

They both stared at poor Zoe, and Bets was almost in tears. Daisy wanted to blurt out about the handkerchief and how she had put the Z on it —but she stopped herself in time. She must ask Fatty's permission first.

'Mr. Goon was most unpleasant,' said Mrs. Thomas. 'He cross-examined me about Zoe till I was tired! He wanted to see all the navy coats in the house too—goodness knows what for!'

The two girls knew quite well! Goon had got that bit of navy-blue cloth that Fatty had jabbed on a nail for a false clue—and he was looking for a coat with a hole in it to match the piece of cloth! Oh dear—this was worse and worse.

'He also wanted to know what kind of cigarettes we smoked,' said Zoe. 'And he seemed awfully pleased when we showed him a boxful—Player's!'

Daisy's heart sank even further, and so did Bets'. It was Player's cigarettes whose ends Fatty had scattered over the verandah. Whoever would have thought that their silly false clues would have fitted so well into this case—and alas, fitted poor Zoe so well!

Bets blinked back her tears. She was scared and unhappy. She looked desperately at Daisy. Daisy

caught the look and knew that Bets wanted to go.
She wanted to go herself, as well. She too was
scared and worried. Fatty must be told all this. He
really must. He would know what to do !

So the two of them got up and said a hurried
good-bye. 'We'll be seeing you this afternoon,'
said Daisy to Zoe. 'We're coming to the show.
Could we have your autograph, all of us, if we wait
at the stage-door ? '

'Of course,' said Zoe. 'How many of you ?
Five ? Right—I'll tell the others, if you like, and
they will all give you their autographs. Mind you
clap me this afternoon ! '

'Oh, we will, we really will,' said Bets, fervently.
'Please don't get arrested, will you ? '

Zoe laughed. 'Of course not. I didn't do the
robbery, and poor Boysie had nothing to do with it
either. I'm quite sure of that. I'm not really afraid
of that nasty Mr. Goon. Don't worry ! '

But the two girls did worry dreadfully as they
hurried away, longing for twelve o'clock to come, so
that they could tell Fatty and the others all that
they had found out.

'We did very well, actually,' said Daisy, when
they got to Bets' playroom and sat down to talk things
over. 'Only we found out things we didn't like
at all. That *handkerchief*, Bets ! I do feel so guilty.
I'll never, never do a thing like that again in my life.'

Larry and Pip came along about ten to twelve.
They looked pleased with themselves.

'Hallo, girls ! How did you get on ? ' said Pip.
'We did very well ! '

So they had. They had biked down to the
Little Theatre, and had gone to the booking-office

to book the seats for the afternoon's show. But the office was closed. Blow!

'Let's snoop round a bit—because if any one sees us, we can always say we've come to buy tickets, and we were looking for some one to ask,' said Pip. So they left the front of the theatre and went round to the back, trying various doors on the way. They were all locked.

They came to the car-park at the back of the theatre. A man was there, cleaning a motor-bicycle. The boys had no idea who he was.

'That's a fine bike,' said Pip to Larry. The man heard their voices, and looked up. He was a middle-aged man, rather stout, with a thin-lipped mouth and bad-temper lines on his forehead.

'What are you doing here?' he said.

'Well, we actually came to buy tickets for this afternoon's show,' said Larry. 'But the booking-office is shut.'

'Of course it is. You can get the tickets when you come along this afternoon,' said the man, rubbing vigorously at the shining mud-guards of the motor-bicycle. 'We only open the booking-office on Saturday mornings, when we expect plenty of people. Anyway, clear off now. I don't like loiterers—after that robbery on Friday I'm not putting up with any one hanging around my theatre!'

'Oh—are you the manager, by any chance?' said Larry, at once.

'Yes. I am. The Man in the News! The man who was doped and robbed last Friday!' said the manager. 'If I could only get my hands on the one who did that job!'

'Have you any idea who did it?' asked Pip.

'WHAT ARE YOU DOING HERE?' HE SAID.
'WELL, WE ACTUALLY CAME TO BUY TICKETS FOR THIS
AFTERNOON'S SHOW,' SAID LARRY.

8

'None at all,' said the manager. 'I don't really believe it was that idiot of a Boysie. He'd never have been able to do all that. Anyway, he's too scared of me to try on tricks of that sort—but he might have helped some one else to do it. Some one he let in that night, when the theatre was empty!'

The boys were thrilled to hear all this first-hand information. 'It said in the paper that Boysie—the Pantomime Cat—brought you in your cup of tea—the one that was drugged,' said Larry. 'Did he, sir?'

'He certainly brought me in the tea,' said the manager. 'I was very busy, and only just glanced up to take it—but it was Boysie all right. He was still in his cat-skin so I couldn't mistake him. Too lazy to take it off. That's Boysie all over. I've even known him go to bed in it. But he's queer in the head, you know. Like a child. He couldn't have done the job by himself, though he must have had something to do with it—he's so easily led.'

'Then—somebody might have come back that night—been let in by Boysie—your tea might have been drugged—and taken up by Boysie to you as usual, so that you wouldn't suspect anything,' said Larry. 'And, as soon as you were asleep, the one that Boysie let in must have crept up to your room, taken down the mirror, got the key from wherever you keep it, and opened the safe—and got away before you woke up.'

'That's about it,' said the manager, standing up to polish the handle-bars. 'And what's more, it must have been one of the cast, because no one knows so much about things as they do—why, whoever the thief was even knew that I didn't keep the safe-key on my key-ring—I always keep it in a secret pocket of my wallet. And only the cast knew that for once in a way I hadn't put Thursday's takings into the Bank, because they saw me coming back in a temper with it, when I found the Bank was closed ! '

The boys drank all this in. Some of it they already knew, but it sounded much more exciting and real to hear it from the lips of the manager himself. They didn't like him—he looked bad-tempered and mean. They could quite well imagine that he would have a lot of enemies who would like to pay him back for some spiteful thing he had said or done to them.

' I suppose the police are on the job all right,' said Pip, taking a duster and beginning to rub up the spokes of the wheels.

' Oh yes. That constable—what's his name—Goon—has been practically *living* here this week-end—interviewing every one. He's got poor Boysie so scared that I don't think he really knows what he's saying now. He shouts at him till Boysie bursts into tears.'

' Beast,' muttered Pip, and the manager looked at him in surprise.

' Oh, I don't know. If Boysie did it, he's got to get it out of him somehow. Anyway, it doesn't hurt him to be yelled at—only way to get things into his thick head sometimes ! '

The bicycle was finished now, and shone brightly. The manager ran it into a shed. ' Well, that's done,' he said. ' Sorry I can't give you your tickets now. You'll get them easily enough this afternoon. There are never many people on Mondays.'

The boys went off, delighted at all they had learnt. To get the whole story from the manager himself was simply marvellous. Now they knew as much as Goon did ! It was certainly very, very mysterious. The Pantomime Cat *had* taken the drugged cup of tea to the manager—and if he hadn't put the sleeping-draught into it himself, he must have known who had done it—must even have let them in. He might even have watched whilst the thief took down the mirror and robbed the safe. Things looked very black for Boysie. Larry and Pip could quite well imagine how Goon must have shouted and yelled at him to try and make him tell the name of the robber.

' Come on—it's a quarter to twelve. Let's get back,' said Larry, who was bursting to tell his news. ' I wonder how the girls have got on. They had an easy job, really. And so had Fatty—just got to pump Pippin, and that's all.'

' I like this detecting business, don't you ? ' said Larry, as they cycled up the road. ' Of course it's more difficult for us than for Goon or Pippin— all they've got to do is to go to any one they like and ask questions, knowing that the people *must* answer the police—and they can go into any house they like and snoop round—but we can't.'

' No, we can't. But on the other hand, we can perhaps pick up little bits of news that people might not tell Goon,' said Pip. ' Look out—there's Goon ! '

So it was—a frowning and majestic Goon, riding his bicycle, and looking very important. He called out to them as he came near.

' Where's that fat boy ? You tell him if I see him again this morning I'll go and complain to his

parents. Poking his Nose where he's not wanted!
Where is he?'

'I don't know,' said Pip and Larry together,
and grinned. What could Fatty have been doing
now?

'You don't know! Gah! I bet you know
where he's hiding, ready to pick Pippin's brains
again. Does he think he's on this Case, too? Well,
he's not. *I'm* in charge of this. You tell him that!'

And with that Mr. Goon sailed off, leaving
Larry and Pip full of curiosity to know what in the
world Fatty had been doing now!

XIV. MORE NEWS—AND A VERY FAT FACE

FATTY had had rather a hectic morning. He had biked down to the road where Goon lived, and had looked into the front room of the police cottage as he passed by. Only Pippin was there. Good.

Fatty leaned his bicycle against the little wall in front of the house, leaving Buster on guard. He then went down the front path, and knocked on the window of the room where Pippin was sitting, laboriously making out reports on this and that.

Pippin looked up and grinned. He opened the door to Fatty and took the boy into the front room.

'Any news?' said Fatty.

'Well,' said Pippin, 'there's a report on the safe and the mirror—about fingerprints. Not a single one to be found!'

'Then whoever did the job was wily,' said Fatty. 'Looks as if that rules out the Pantomime Cat!'

Pippin was about to speak again, when he heard Buster barking. They both looked out of the window. Goon was just dismounting from his bicycle, looking as black as thunder. Buster parked himself in the middle of the gateway, and barked deliriously, as if to say, 'Yah! Can't come in! Woof, woof! Can't come in! Yah!'

'You'd better go,' said Pippin, hurriedly. 'I've a bit more news for you but you must go now.'

As Buster now showed every sign of being about to attack Goon, Fatty hurriedly left the house and ran up to the front gate. He picked Buster up and put him in his bicycle basket.

'What you doing here?' blustered Goon. 'I've warned Pippin against you, Mr. Nosey Parker. You won't get anything out of *him*! He's not on this case. He doesn't know a thing—and he wouldn't tell you if he did. Clear-orf! I'm tired of that fat face of yours.'

'Don't be rude, Mr. Goon,' said Fatty, with dignity. He hated his face to be called fat.

'Rude! I'm not rude—just truthful,' said Mr. Goon, wheeling his bicycle in at the gate. 'I tell you, I don't want to see that fat face of yours any more to-day! I'm a busy man, with important things to do. I won't have you noseying around.'

He went in, pleased to think that Pippin had heard him treat that fat boy in the way he ought to be treated. Aha! He, Mr. Goon, was well on the way to solving a Very Difficult Case. Got it all Pat, he had—and for once in a way Master Frederick Algernon Trotteville was going to have his nose put out of joint. Him and his fat face!

With these pleasant thoughts to keep him company Mr. Goon went in to fire off a few sharp remarks at Pippin. Fatty, anxious to have a few more words with Pippin, rode up the road a little way, and then leaned his bicycle against a tree, putting himself the other side of the trunk so that he might watch unseen for Goon to come out and ride off again. The policeman had left his bicycle against the wall of his cottage, as if he meant to come out again in a little while.

Fatty stood and brooded over Goon's rude remarks about the fatness of his face. Goon thought he had a fat face, did he? All right—he'd show him one! Fatty slipped his hand into his pocket and brought out two nice new plump cheek-pads. He slipped one into each cheek, between his teeth and the fleshy part of the cheek. At once he took on a most swollen, blown-out look.

Goon came out of his house in a few minutes, and mounted his bicycle. He rode slowly up the road. Fatty came out from behind his tree to show himself to Goon.

'You here again?' began Goon, wobbling in rage. 'You . . .'

And then he caught sight of Fatty's enormously blown-out cheeks. He blinked and looked again. Fatty grinned, and his cheeks almost burst.

Mr. Goon got off his bicycle, unable to believe his eyes, but Fatty jumped on his and sailed away. He waited in a side-road, riding up and down, till he thought Goon must have gone, and then cycled back to Pippin.

'It's all right,' said Pippin, from the window. 'He's gone to send a telegram off, and after that he's going to the Theatre car-park to snoop round again, and then he's got to go to Loo Farm about a dog. He won't be back for some time.'

Fatty had now taken out his cheek-pads and looked quite normal again.

'I won't keep you more than a few minutes,' he told Pippin. 'I know you're busy. What other news have you?'

'Well, there *was* a sleeping-draught in that cup all right,' said Pippin. 'A harmless one, but strong. Traces of it were found in the cup. So that's proved allright.'

' Anything else ? ' enquired Fatty. ' Has the money been traced ? '

' No. And it won't be either,' said Pippin,' It was all in ten-shilling or pound notes, and silver.'

' Any idea yet who did the job ? ' asked Fatty.

' Well, I've seen Goon's notes, and if you want a *motive* for the robbery—some one with a spite against the manager—any of the company would do for the thief ! ' said Pippin. ' Mr. Goon wasn't going to tell me anything, as you know, but he's so proud of himself for finding out so much, that he gave me his notes to read. Said it would do me good to see how an expert got to work on a case like this ! '

Fatty grinned. ' Yes—sort of thing he *would* say. But what do you mean—all the company had a spite against the manager ? '

' Mr. Goon interviewed the manager, and got quite a lot out of him,' said Pippin. ' Now—take Miss Zoe Markham—she had a row with him that morning and got the sack. And now Lucy White —asked him to lend her some money because her mother was ill, and he raged at her and refused. And here's Peter Watting and William Orr—they want to do a series of decent straight plays here instead of this comic stuff, and the manager laughed at them —told them they were only fit for third-rate comedy stuff. Said that third-rate people would have to be content with third-rate shows.'

' I bet they were angry,' said Fatty.

' Yes. They were furious, apparently,' said Pippin. ' Almost came to blows. Threatened to knock him down if he called them third-rate again. As a matter of fact they are quite good, especially William Orr.'

'Go on,' said Fatty. 'This is interesting. Who else has a grudge against him?'

'John James wanted a rise in his salary,' said Pippin. 'Apparently the manager had promised him this after a six months' run. So he asked for it and was refused. The manager says he never promised him anything of the sort.'

'Nice amiable chap, this manager,' said Fatty with a grin. 'Always ready to help! My word, what a way to run a company! They must all hate him.'

'They do!' said Pippin. 'Even poor Boysie, the Pantomime Cat, detests him. Now let me see —is that the lot? No—here's Alec Grant. He wanted permission to go and act in another show on the days he's not on here—and the manager wouldn't let him. There was an awful row about that, apparently—so, you see, there are plenty of people who would very much like to pay the manager out for his spiteful treatment of them!'

'What about their alibis?' asked Fatty, after a pause to digest all this.

'All checked,' said Pippin. 'And all correct, except that there's a query about Zoe Markham, because she went out of her sister's house that evening, and nobody saw her come back; she says she went straight up to her room. So, what with that fact and the Z on the handkerchief found on the verandah, Goon's got her and Boysie down as Chief Suspects now!'

This wasn't very pleasant. Pippin bent over his papers. 'Well,' he said, 'that's all I can tell you for the present—and don't you let on I've told you, either! You'd better go now—and don't forget to let me know if *you've* got anything interesting up your sleeve.'

' I haven't at the moment,' said Fatty, soberly. ' Except that I hope Mr. Goon was tired after his afternoon walk yesterday ! '

Pippin looked up at once. ' What—trailing that red-headed foreigner ! You don't mean to say he was *you* ! '

' Well—I thought Mr. Goon might as well meet *somebody* off the three-thirty train ! ' said Fatty. ' You'd have thought he would have been a bit suspicious of red-heads by now, wouldn't you, Pippin ? '

And with that Fatty went off whistling on his bicycle, thinking hard. A thought struck him. He put his cheek-pads in, and rode off to the post office. Goon might still be there.

He was. Fatty sidled into the near-by telephone kiosk as Goon came out of the post office. The policeman saw some one grinning at him from the kiosk, and stopped. He gazed in horror at Fatty, whose cheeks were now as enormous as when Goon had seen him a short time before.

Fatty nodded and grinned amiably. Goon walked off, puzzled. That boy ! His face seemed fatter than ever. He couldn't be blowing it out with his breath, because he was grinning. He must have some disease !

Fatty shot off on his bicycle, taking a short cut to the car-park behind the theatre. He took his bike to the shed, and bent over it. In a moment or two Goon came sailing in on *his* bicycle, and dismounted to put it into the shed. He saw a boy there, but took no notice—till Fatty turned round and presented him with yet another wonderful view of his great fat face.

Goon got a shock. He peered closely at Fatty. 'You got toothache?' he enquired. 'Talk about a fat face!'

He disappeared into the theatre, and Fatty rode off to Loo Farm. He waited there for ten minutes, sitting on his bicycle behind a wall. When he spotted Goon coming along, he rode out suddenly, and once again Mr. Goon got a fine view of a full-moon face shining out at him.

'Now you clear-orf!' yelled Mr. Goon. 'Following me about like this! You with your fat face and all. You go and see a dentist. Gah! Think yourself funny following me about with that face.'

'But Mr. Goon—it looks as if you're following *me* about,' protested Fatty. 'I go to telephone, and you are there! I go to the car-park and you come there too. And I call at Loo Farm, and hey, presto, you come along here as well! What are you following ME for? Do you think *I* did the robbery at the Little Theatre?'

Mr. Goon looked in puzzled distaste at Fatty's fat face. He couldn't make it out. How could any one's face get as fat as that so suddenly? Was he seeing double?

He decided not to call at Loo Farm whilst that boy was hanging round with his full-moon face. Mr. Goon rode away down the road, defeated.

'Toad!' he murmured to himself. 'Regular toad, that boy. No doing anything with him. Well, he don't know how well I've got on with this Case. Give him a shock when he finds it's all cleared up, arrests been made, and sees the Inspector giving me a Pat on the Back ! Him and his fat face ! '

Fatty looked at his watch. It was getting on for twelve. He'd better go back and join the others. What news had they been able to get ?

He rode up to Pip's house. They were all there, waiting for him. Bets waved out of the window.

' Buck *up*, Fatty ! We've all got plenty of news ! We thought you were *never* coming ! '

XV. AT THE SHOW—AND AFTERWARDS

THE children sat down in Pip's big playroom, a bag of chocolates between them, supplied by Larry.

'Well—it looks as if we've all got something to report,' said Fatty. 'Girls first. How did you get on, Daisy and Bets?'

Taking it in turns to supply the news, Bets and Daisy told their story. 'Wasn't it *lucky* to see Zoe herself?' said Daisy. 'She's sweet, she really is. *She* couldn't possibly have done the job, Fatty.'

'But isn't it awful about the hanky with Z on?' said Bets. 'And oh, Fatty—she smokes the same kind of cigarettes as our cigarette-ends were made of—Player's!'

'Well, Goon will probably find that most of the others smoke them too, so we needn't worry so much about that,' said Fatty. 'I'm sorry about that hanky business, though. *Why* did we put Z on that silly hanky!'

'Don't you think we ought to tell Goon that—I mean, about us putting the hanky down for a false clue?' said Daisy, anxiously. 'I can't bear Goon going after poor Zoe with a false clue like that—it's awful for her.'

'It can't *prove* anything,' said Fatty, thinking hard. 'If it *had* been hers, she might have dropped it any old time, not just that evening. I don't see that Goon can make it really *prove* anything.'

'Neither do I,' said Larry. 'We'll own up when the case is finished—but I don't see much point in us spoiling our own chances of solving the mystery by confessing to Goon.'

'All right,' said Daisy. 'Only I can't *help* feeling awful about it.'

'I must say you two girls did very well,' said Fatty. 'You got a lot of most interesting information. What about you, Larry and Pip?'

Then Larry and Pip told of their meeting with the manager, and related in great detail all he had said to them. Fatty listened eagerly. This was splendid!

'I say—that was fine,' he said when the two boys had finished. 'I feel there's absolutely no doubt at all now that it was Boysie who took in the doped tea. Well—if he *did* do the job—or helped somebody to do it—he certainly made it quite clear that he was in it, by taking the tea to the manager! I suppose he didn't realize that the remains of the tea would show the traces of the sleeping-draught. It's the sort of thing a mutt like Boysie would forget.'

'Well—we shall see him this afternoon,' said Daisy. 'I forgot to tell you, Fatty, that we arranged with Zoe to meet all the members of the show after it had finished this afternoon, for autographs. So we shall see Boysie as well.'

'Very good,' said Fatty, pleased. 'You all seem to have done marvellously. I consider I've trained you jolly well!'

He was well pummelled for that remark. When peace had been restored again, Larry asked him how *he* had got on—and he related all that Pippin had told him.

'It's funny that every single member of the show had a grudge against the manager, isn't it?'

he said. ' He must be a beast. He did just the kind of things that would make people want to pay him back. Motives sticking out everywhere ! '

' What are motives ? ' Bets wanted to know.

' Good reasons for doing something,' explained Fatty. ' Understand ? The show-people all had good reasons for getting back at their manager— motives for paying him out for his beastliness.'

' It's a very interesting mystery, this,' said Larry. ' Seven people could have done the job—all of them have good motives for getting even with the manager —and all of them, except Boysie, and perhaps Zoe, have good alibis. And we don't think either of those would have done the job ! Zoe sounds much too nice.'

' I agree,' said Fatty. ' It's a super mystery. A proper Who-Dun-It.'

' What's *that* ? ' said Bets at once.

' Oh dear—Bets is an awful baby,' said Pip. ' Bets—a Who-Dun-It is a mystery with a crime in it that people have got to solve—to find out who did it.'

' Well, what's it called a Who-Dun-It for, then ? ' said Bets, sensibly. ' I shall call it a Who-Did-It.'

' You call it what you like,' said Fatty, grinning. ' So long as we find out who-dun-it or who-did-it, it doesn't matter what we call it. Now—what's the next step ? '

' We'll all go to the show this afternoon, watch every one acting, and then go round and collect autographs, speak to all the members of the show, and take particular notice of Boysie,' said Larry, at once.

' Go up top,' said Fatty. ' And to-morrow we go

after the rest of the alibis.   Larry and Daisy will
go to see Mary Adams, to find out if Lucy White's
alibi is sound—and Pip and I will see if we can test
Peter Watting's and William Orr's.   We shall have
to find out how to check John James too—he went
to the cinema all the evening—or so he said.'

'Yes—and Alec Grant's,' said Daisy.   'He went
to Sheepridge and gave a show there on his own.'

'Silly to check that, really,' said Pip.   'So many
people heard and saw him.   Anyway, it will be jolly
easy to check.'

'There's the dinner-bell,' said Pip.   'I must
go and wash.   What time do we meet this afternoon?
And where?   Down at the theatre?'

'Yes,' said Fatty.   'Be there at a quarter to three.
The show starts at three.   So long!'

They were all very hungry indeed for their meal.
Detecting was hungry work, it seemed!   Fatty spent
a good time after his meal writing out all the things
he knew about the mystery.   It made very interesting
reading indeed.   Fatty read it over afterwards, and
felt puzzled.   So many Suspects, so many motives,
so many alibis—how in the world would they ever
unravel them all?

At a quarter to three all the Find-Outers were
down at the Little Theatre.   A grubby little boy was
in the booking-office, and gave them their tickets.
They passed into the theatre and found their seats.
They had taken them as far forward as they could,
so as to be able to observe the actors very closely.

They were in the middle of the second row—
very good places indeed.   Some one was playing the
piano softly.   There was no band, of course, for the
show was only a small one.   The stage-curtain

9

shook a little in the draughts that came in each time
the door was opened. The children gazed at it,
admiring the marvellous sunset depicted on the
great sheet.

The show began punctually. The curtain went
up exactly at three o'clock, and the audience sat up
in expectation.

There were two plays and a skit on Dick Whittington's Pantomime. In the first two plays, Boysie
did not appear, but he came in at the last one, and
the children shouted with delight as he shuffled in
on all fours, dressed in the big furry skin that the
boys had seen through the window on Friday night.

He was very funny. He waved to the children
just as he had waved to the three boys when they
had peered in to see him on the Friday night. He
capered about, cuddled up to Zoe Markham (who
was Dick Whittington and looked very fine indeed),
and was altogether quite a success.

' Zoe looks lovely,' said Larry.

' Yes—but why do the Principal Boys' parts
always have to be taken by girls,' said Daisy, in the
interval of a change of scenery. ' Do you remember,
in Aladdin, it was a girl who took Aladdin's part
—and in Cinderella a girl took the part of the Prince.'

' Sh ! ' said Bets. ' The curtain is going up again.
Oh, there's the Cat ! And oh, look—his skin is
splitting down by his tail ! '

So it was. The Cat seemed to realize this and
kept feeling the hole with his front paw. ' Meeow,'
he said, ' meeow ! ' Almost as if he was a real cat,
dismayed at the splitting of his coat !

' I hope he doesn't split it all the way down,'
said Bets. ' I bet he'd get into a row with that awful

manager, if he did. Oh, isn't he funny! He's
pretending to go after a mouse. *Is* it a mouse ? '

'Only a clockwork one,' said Daisy. 'Well,
Boysie may be queer in his head and all that—but I
think he's jolly clever in his acting. I do really.'

Fatty thought so too. He was wondering if
any one quite so good at acting could be as silly as
people said. Well—he would see if he could talk
to Boysie afterwards—then he could make up his
own mind about him.

The show came to an end. The curtain came
down, went up once, and came down again. It
stayed down. Every one clapped and then got up
to go home. It was past five o'clock.

'Now let's rush round to the stage-door,' said
Fatty. 'Come on ! '

So, autograph-books in hand, the five of them tore
round to the stage-door, anxious to catch all the
actors and actresses before they left.

They waited for five minutes. Then Zoe came
to the door, still with some of the grease-paint on
her pretty face. But she had changed into a suit
now, and looked quite different.

'Come along in and meet the others inside,'
she said. ' They won't be out for a few minutes and
it's cold standing at that door.'

So, feeling a little nervous, the five children
trooped in at the stage-door and followed Zoe to a
big room, where one or two of the actors were gulping
down cups of tea.

Peter Watting and William Orr were there,
one elderly and rather sour-looking, one young and
rather miserable-looking. They didn't look nearly
so fine as they had done on the stage, when Peter

had been Dick's master and William had been a very dashing captain, singing a loud, jolly song of the sea, the blue blue sea !

They nodded at the children. 'Hallo, kids ! Autograph-hunting ? Well, we're flattered, I'm sure ! Hand over your books.'

The two men scribbled in each book. Then Zoe introduced them to Lucy White, a tall, gentle-looking girl who had been Dick Whittington's sweetheart in the play. She had looked really beautiful on the stage, with a great mass of flowing golden curls, which the children had admired very much. But the mass of curls now stood on a side-table—a grand wig—and Lucy was seen to be a quiet, brown-haired girl with a rather worried face.

She signed the books too. Then John James came in, burly, dour, and heavy-footed, a big man, just right for the black king in the play. 'Hallo ! ' he said. ' You don't mean to say that somebody wants our autographs ! Well, well ! Here's fame for you ! '

He signed the books too. Fatty began to get into conversation with William and Peter. Larry tried to talk to John James. Pip looked round. Surely there should be somebody else to ask to sign their books ?

There was—and he came in at that moment, a small, dapper little man, who had played the part of Dick's mother on the stage. He had been very good as the mother—neat and nimble, using an amusing high voice, and even singing two or three songs in a woman's voice very cleverly indeed.

' Could we have your autograph, please ? ' said Fatty, going up to him. ' I say, I did like your performance. I could have sworn you were a woman! Even your voice ! '

' Yes—Alec was in great form with his singing to-day,' said Zoe. ' Got his high notes beautifully ! You should see him imitate me and Lucy—takes us off really well, so that you'd hardly know it wasn't us ! We tell him he's lost in this little company. He ought to be on in the West End ! '

' He thinks that himself, don't you, Alec ? ' said John James, in a slightly mocking voice. ' But the manager doesn't agree with him.'

' Don't talk to me about *him*,' said Alec. ' We all detest the fellow. Here you are, kids—catch ! And I hope you can read my signature ! '

He threw them their books. Fatty opened his and saw a most illegible scrawl that he could just make out to be ' Alec Grant '—but only just.

Zoe laughed. ' He always writes like that. Nobody can ever read his writing. I tell him he might just as well write " Hot Potatoes " or " Peppermint Creams " and nobody would know the difference. I wonder your mother can ever read your letters, Alec.'

' She can't,' said Alec. ' She waits till I get home and then she gets me to read them to her. And I can't ! '

Every one laughed. ' Well, so long,' said Alec, winding a yellow scarf round his neck. ' See you to-morrow. And, mind you none of you knock the manager on the head to-night ! '

XVI. THE PANTOMIME CAT HAS A TEA-PARTY

THE children thought they ought to go too. Fatty felt as if they had stayed too long already. Then he remembered something.

'Oh—what about the Pantomime Cat? We haven't got *his* autograph. Where is he?'

'Clearing up the stage, I expect,' said Zoe. 'That's one of his jobs. But he won't sign your albums for you—poor old Boysie can't write.'

'Can't he, *really*?' said Bets, in amazement. 'But I thought he was grown-up—isn't he?'

'Yes—he's twenty-four,' said Zoe. 'But he's like a kid of six. He can hardly read, either. But he's a dear, he really is. I'll go and get him for you.'

But before she could go, the Pantomime Cat came in. He walked on his hind legs, and had thrown back the furry cat-skin head, so that it looked like a grotesque hood.

He had a big head, small eyes, set too close together, teeth that stuck out in front like a rabbit's, and a very scared expression on his face.

He came up to Zoe and put his hand in hers like a child. 'Zoe,' he said. 'Zoe must help Boysie.'

'What is it, Boysie?' said Zoe, speaking as if Boysie was a child. 'Tell Zoe.'

'Look,' said Boysie, and turned himself round dolefully. Every one looked—and saw a big split in poor Boysie's cat-skin, near the tail.   It had got much bigger since Bets had noticed it.

'And look,' said Boysie, pointing to a split down his tummy.   'Zoe can mend it for Boysie?'

'Yes, Boysie, of course,' said Zoe, kindly, and the Cat slipped his hand in hers again, smiling up at her.   He only reached to her shoulder.   'You're getting fat, Boysie,' said Zoe.   'Eating too much, and splitting your skin!'

Boysie now saw the children for the first time and smiled at them with real pleasure.   'Children,' he said, pointing at them.   'Why are they here?'

'They came to talk to us, Boysie,' said Zoe. ('He wouldn't understand what I mean if I said you wanted autographs,' she whispered to Fatty.)

Peter Watting and William Orr, tall and thin, now said good-bye and went.   Lucy White followed, leaving her wig of golden curls behind.   Boysie put it on and ran round the room, grinning, looking perfectly dreadful.

'See?   He's just like a six-year old, isn't he?' said Zoe.   'But he's so simple and kind—does anything he can for any of us.   He's very clever with his fingers—he can carve wood beautifully. Look—here are some of the things Boysie has done for me.'

She took down a row of small wooden animals, most beautifully carved.   Boysie, still in his golden wig, came and stood by them, smiling with pleasure.

'Boysie!   I think they're *beautiful*.' said Bets, overcome with admiration.   'How *do* you do such lovely carving?   Oh, *look* at this little lamb—it's perfect.'

Boysie suddenly ran out of the room.   He came

back with another little lamb, rather like the one
Bets admired. He pressed it into her hand, smiling
foolishly, his small eyes full of tears.

'You have this,' he said. 'I like you.'

Bets turned and looked at him. She did not
see the ugly face, the too-close eyes, the big-toothed
mouth. She only saw the half-scared kindness
that lay behind them all. She gave him a sudden
hug, thinking of him as if he were a child much
younger and smaller than herself.

'There! See how pleased the little girl is,' said
Zoe. 'That's nice of you, Boysie.'

She turned to the others. 'He's always like
that,' she said. 'He'd give away the shirt off his
back if he could. You can't help liking him, can
you?'

'No,' said every one, and it was true. Boysie
was queer in the head and silly, he was ugly to look
at—but he was kind and sincere and humble, he
had a sense of fun—and you simply *couldn't* help
liking him.

'I can't bear it when people are unkind to Boysie,'
said Zoe. 'Sometimes the manager is, and I just
see red then. I did last Friday, didn't I, Boysie?'

Boysie's face clouded over and he nodded.
'You mustn't go away,' he said to Zoe, and put his
hand in hers. 'You mustn't leave Boysie.'

'He says that because the manager gave me
notice on Friday,' said Zoe. 'He's afraid I'll go.
But I shan't. The manager won't want to lose me
really—though I'd like a bit of a rest. But he said
this afternoon he didn't mean what he said last
Friday. He's a funny one. Nobody likes him.'

'I say—I suppose we really ought to go,' said

Fatty. 'Are you coming, Zoe—may we call you Zoe ? '

'Of course,' said Zoe. 'Well, no, I won't go yet. I must mend Boysie's cat-skin. I'll stay and have tea with him, I think. I say, Boysie—shall we ask all these nice children to stay to tea too ? '

Boysie was thrilled. He stroked Zoe's arm, and then took Bets' hand. 'Boysie will make tea,' he said. 'You sit down.'

'Boysie, aren't you going to take off your cat-skin ? ' asked Zoe. 'You'll be so hot—and you might split it even more.'

Boysie paid no attention. He went off into a small cupboard-like place, and they heard him filling a kettle.

'We'd *love* to stay,' said Fatty, who thought Zoe was just about the nicest person he had ever seen. 'If we're no bother. Shall I pop out and buy some buns ? '

'Yes. That would be a lovely idea,' said Zoe. 'Where's my purse. I'll give you the money.'

'I've plenty, thank you,' said Fatty, hastily. 'I won't be long ! Coming, Larry ? '

He and Larry disappeared. Boysie watched for the kettle to boil, which it soon did. Just as he turned off the gas Fatty and Larry came back with a collection of jammy buns, chocolate cakes and ginger biscuits.

'There's a plate in the cupboard where Boysie is,' said Zoe. 'My word—what a feast ! '

Fatty went into the little cupboard. He watched Boysie with interest. The little fellow, still in his cat-skin, had warmed the brown teapot. He now tipped out the water from the pot and put in some tea.

' How many spoons of tea, Zoe ? ' he called.

' Oh, four will do,' said Zoe. ' Count them for him, will you—he can't count very well.'

' I can count four,' said Boysie, indignantly, but proceeded to put five in, instead. Then he poured boiling water into the pot and put on the lid.

' Do you make tea every evening ? ' asked Fatty, and Boysie nodded.

' Yes. He's good at making tea,' said Zoe, as Boysie carried the teapot in and set it down on the table. ' He usually makes it for us as soon as the show is over—and then he makes some for the manager much later. Don't you, Boysie ? '

To the children's alarm Boysie suddenly burst into tears. ' I didn't take him his tea. I didn't,' he wept.

' He's remembering about last Friday,' said Zoe, patting Boysie comfortingly. ' That policeman keeps on and on at him, trying to make him say he took a cup of tea to the manager and Boysie keeps saying he didn't. Though the manager says he *did*. I expect Boysie has got muddled and has forgotten.'

' Tell us about it, Boysie,' said Fatty, rather thrilled at getting so much first-hand information. ' You don't need to worry about talking to *us*. We're your friends. We know you didn't have anything to do with what happened on Friday night.'

' I didn't, did I ? ' said Boysie, looking at Zoe. ' You all went, Zoe. You didn't stay with Boysie like to-day. I was in my cat-skin because it's hard to take off by myself. You know it is. And I went into the back room where there's a fire ! '

' He means the room behind the verandah,'

'AND I SAW YOU—AND YOU—AND YOU,' SAID BOYSIE, SURPRIS-
INGLY, POKING HIS PAW AT FATTY, LARRY, AND PIP.

explained Zoe. 'There's an electric fire there that Boysie likes to sit by.'

'And I saw you—and you—and you,' said Boysie, surprisingly, poking his paw at Fatty, Larry, and Pip. 'Not you,' he added, poking Bets and Daisy.

'You never said that before,' said Zoe, in surprise. 'That's naughty, Boysie. You *didn't* see these children.'

'I did. They looked in the window,' said Boysie. 'I looked at them too. I frightened them! They looked again and I waved to them to tell them not to be frightened, because they are nice children.'

The five children looked at one another. *They* knew that Boysie was telling the truth. He *had* seen them that Friday night—he *had* waved to them.

'Did you tell the policeman this?' asked Fatty, suddenly.

Boysie shook his head. 'No. Boysie didn't remember then. Remembers now.'

'What did you do after the children had gone?' asked Fatty, gently.

'I made some tea,' said Boysie, screwing up his face to remember. 'Some for me and some for the manager.'

'Did you drink yours first?' asked Fatty. 'Or did you take *his* up first?'

'Mine was hot,' said Boysie. 'Very hot. Too hot. I played till it was cool, then I drank it.'

'*Then* did you pour out the manager's tea and take it to him?' asked Fatty. Boysie blinked his eyes and a hunted look came over his face.

'No,' he said. 'No, no, no! I didn't take it, I

didn't, I didn't! I was tired. I lay down on the rug and I went to sleep. But I didn't take the tea upstairs. Don't make me say I did. I didn't, I didn't.'

There was a long pause. Every one was wondering what to say. Fatty spoke first.

'Have a jammy bun, every one? Here, Boysie, there's an extra-jammy one for you—and don't you bother any more about that tea. Forget it!'

NO more was said about Friday evening after that.
It was quite clear that talking about it upset Boysie
terribly. Fatty was very puzzled indeed. Boysie
had taken up the tea—the manager said so quite
definitely, because, as now, he was still in his cat-
skin and was quite unmistakable. Then what
was the point of Boysie denying it ? Was he trying
to shield somebody, in his foolish way, by denying
everything to do with the doped cup of tea ?

If so—who was he trying to shield ? Zoe ?
No ! Nobody could possibly suspect Zoe of drugging
any one's tea, or robbing a safe. Nobody—except
Goon !

It was imperative to check up all the other
alibis. If there was a single chink in any of them,
that was probably the person Boysie was trying to
shield. Fatty made up his mind that every other
alibi must be gone into the next day without fail.
If he couldn't find something definite, it looked as
if the poor old Pantomime Cat would be arrested,
and Zoe too ! Because Goon would be sure that
Zoe, whom Boysie obviously adored, was the person
he was shielding.

It was a curious tea-party, but the children
enjoyed it. Towards the end, a loud voice came
down the stairs outside the room.

' What's all the row down there ? Who's there ?
I can hear *your* voice, Zoe ! '

Zoe went to the door. ' Yes, I'm here. I'm
stopping behind to mend Boysie's cat-skin. It's

all split. And there are a few children here, too, who came for our autographs. They're having a cup of tea with me and Boysie.'

'You tell them to be careful Boysie doesn't put something in their tea, then!' shouted the manager, and went back to his room, banging the door loudly.

'Pleasant fellow, isn't he?' said Larry. 'We met him this morning. A very nasty bit of work.'

'I couldn't agree more,' said Zoe. 'Well, dears, you'd better go. Get out of your skin, Boysie, if you want me to mend it.'

The children said good-bye, shaking hands with both Zoe and Boysie. Boysie looked intensely pleased at all this ceremony. He bowed each time he shook hands.

'A pleasure,' he said to each of them. 'A pleasure!'

They all went to get their bikes, which they had left in the stand inside the shed. 'Well! Fancy getting asked inside, meeting every one, and having tea with Zoe and Boysie!' said Fatty, pleased.

'Yes. And hearing his own story,' said Larry, pushing his bike out into the yard. 'Do you believe him, Fatty?'

'Well, I know it's quite impossible that he shouldn't have taken in that cup of tea, but yet I feel Boysie's speaking the truth,' said Fatty. 'I've never been so puzzled in my life. One minute I think one thing and the next I think another.'

'Well, *Zoe* didn't do it,' said Bets, loyally. 'She's much, much, much too nice.'

'I agree with you,' said Fatty. 'She couldn't have done that robbery any more than *you* could, Bets. Well, we must look elsewhere, that's all. We must check all the rest of the alibis to-morrow without fail.'

So the next morning the Find-Outers started off with their checking. Larry and Daisy set off to Mary Adams' flat, to find out about the gentle Lucy White. Fatty and Pip went off by the river, to find The Turret and discover if William Orr and Peter Watting *had* been there on Friday night, as they said.

'Then we'll check up on John James and the cinema if we can this afternoon,' said Fatty, 'and on Alec Grant as well, if we've time. We'll have to look lively now, because it seems to me that Goon will move soon. If he sees that poor Boysie any more he'll send him *right* off his head!'

Daisy found a half-embroidered cushion-case which she had never finished. She took the silks that went with it and wrapped the whole lot up in a parcel. 'Come along,' she said to Larry. 'We'll soon find out about Lucy White—though, honestly, I think it's waste of time checking *her* alibi. She doesn't look as if she could say boo to a goose!'

They arrived at Mary Adams' flat and went up-stairs to her front door. They rang, and the old lady opened the door.

'Well, well, well—*what* a surprise,' she said, pleased. 'Miss Daisy *and* Master Larry. It's a long time since I've seen you—what enormous children you've grown. You come along in.'

She led the way into her tiny sitting-room. She took down a tin of chocolate biscuits from the mantelpiece and offered them one. She was a small, white-haired old lady, almost crippled with rheuma-tism now, but still able to sew and knit.

Daisy opened her parcel. ' Mary, do you think you could possibly finish this cushion-case for me before Easter ? I want to give it to mother, and I know I shan't have time to finish it myself, because I'm embroidering her some hankies too. How much would you charge for doing it for me ? '

' Not a penny, Miss Daisy,' said Mary Adams, beaming. ' It would be a pleasure to do something for you, and especially something that's going to be given to your dear mother. Bless your dear heart, I'd love to finish it just for love and nothing else.'

' Thank you *awfully*, Mary,' said Daisy. ' It's very kind of you—and I'll bring you some of our daffodils as soon as they're properly out. They're awfully behind this year.'

' Have another biscuit ? ' said Mary, taking down the tin again. ' Well, it *is* nice to see you both. I've been ill, you know, and haven't been out much. So it's a real change to see a visitor or two.'

Here was just the opening they wanted !

' Do you know Lucy White ? ' said Larry. ' We got her autograph this afternoon. She's a friend of yours, isn't she ? '

' Yes—dear Lucy ! She came to see me every night last week, when I was bad,' said Mary. ' I had a lot of knitting to finish and that kind girl came in and helped me till it was all done.'

' Did she come on Friday too ? ' asked Daisy.

' Ah—you're like that Mr. Goon—he's been round here three times asking questions about Friday evening,' said Mary. ' Yes, Lucy came along about a quarter to six, and we sat and knitted till half-past nine, when she went home. We heard the nine o'clock news, and she made us some cocoa,

10

with some biscuits, and we had *such* a nice time together.'

Well, that seemed pretty definite.

' Didn't Lucy leave you at all, till half-past nine ? ' said Daisy.

' Not once. She didn't so much as go out of the room,' said Mary. ' There we sat in our chairs, knitting away for dear life—and the next day Lucy took all the knitting we'd done that week, and delivered it for me. She's a good kind girl.'

There came a ring at the door. ' I'll go for you,' said Daisy and got up. She opened the door—and there was Mr. Goon, red in the face from climbing the steps to Mary's flat ! He glared suspiciously at Daisy.

' What are *you* doing here ? ' he demanded. ' Poking your noses in ? '

' We came to ask Mary to do some sewing,' said Daisy, in a dignified voice.

' *Ho* yes ! ' said Mr. Goon, disbelievingly. ' Mary Adams in ? '

' Yes I am,' called Mary Adams' voice, sounding rather cross. ' Is that you again, Mr. Goon ? I've nothing more to say to you. Please go away. Wasting my time like this ! '

' I just want to ask you a few more questions,' said Mr. Goon, walking into the little sitting-room.

' Theophilus Goon, since you were a nasty little boy *so* high, you've always been a one for asking snoopy questions,' said Mary Adams, and the two children heard Mr. Goon snort angrily. They called good-bye and fled away, laughing.

' I bet he *was* a nasty little boy too ! ' said Larry, as they went down the stairs. ' Well, that was easy, Daisy.'

'Very,' said Daisy. 'And quite definite too. It rules out Lucy White. I do wonder how the others are getting on.'

Bets was waiting at home with Buster. She had wanted to go with Pip and Fatty, but Fatty had said no, she had better stay with Buster. He and Pip had gone off down by the river, taking the road along which William Orr and Peter Watting had said they went.

They came to a tall and narrow house, with a little turret. On the gate was its name. 'The Turret. Coffee, sandwiches, snacks.'

'Well, here we are,' said Fatty. 'We'll try the coffee, sandwiches, snacks. I feel jolly hungry.'

So in they went and found a nice table looking out on a primrosey garden. A small girl came to serve them. She didn't look more than about twelve, though she must have been a good deal older.

'Coffee for two, please,' said Fatty. 'And sandwiches. And something snacky.'

The girl laughed. 'I'll bring you a tray of snacks,' she said. 'Then you can help yourselves.'

She brought them two cups of hot, steaming coffee, a plate of egg, potted meat, and cress sandwiches, and a tray of delicious-looking snacks.

'Ha! *We've* chosen the right place to come and check up on alibis,' said Fatty, eyeing the tray with delight. 'Look at all this!'

The boys ate the sandwiches, and then chose a snack. It was delicious. 'Come on—let's carry on with the snacks,' said Fatty. 'We've had a long walk and I'm hungry. I don't care if I *do* spoil my dinner—it's a jolly good way to spoil it— most enjoyable.'

'But have you got enough money to pay, Fatty?' asked Larry, anxiously. 'I haven't got much on me.'

'Plenty,' said the wealthy Fatty, and rattled his pockets. 'We'll start on checking the alibi as soon as we've finished our meal. Hallo—LOOK who's here!'

It was Goon! He walked in as if he owned the place, and then he saw Fatty!

XVIII. MORE CHECKING—AND A FEW SNACKS

MR. GOON advanced on Fatty's table. 'Everywhere I go,' boomed Mr. Goon, 'I see some of you kids. Now, what are you doing *here*?'

'Snacking,' said Fatty, politely. 'Did you come in for a snack too, Mr. Goon? Not much left, unfortunately.'

'You hold your tongue,' said Mr. Goon.

'But you asked me a question,' objected Fatty. 'You said . . .'

'I know what I said,' said Mr. Goon. 'I'm Fed Up with you kids! I go to Mary Adams and I see some of you there. I come here and here you are again. And I bet when I go somewhere else you'll be there as well! Lot of pests you are.'

'It's funny how often we see *you* too, Mr. Goon,' said Fatty, in the pleasant, polite voice that always infuriated Mr. Goon. 'Quite a treat.'

Mr. Goon swelled up and his face went purple. Then the little girl came into the room, and he turned to her pompously. 'Is your mother in? I want a word with her.'

'No, she's not, sir,' said the little girl. 'I'm the only one here. Mother will be back soon, if you like to wait.'

'I can't wait,' said Mr. Goon, annoyed. 'Too much to do. I'll come to-morrow.'

He was just going when he turned to look at Fatty. He had suddenly remembered his fat cheeks. They didn't seem nearly so fat now.

'What you done to make your cheeks thin?' he said, suspiciously.

'Well—I *might* have had all my back teeth out,' said Fatty. 'Let me see—did I, Larry? Do you remember?'

'Gah!' said Mr. Goon, and went. The little girl laughed uproariously.

'Oh, you are funny!' she said. 'You really are. Isn't he horrid? He came and asked Mother and me ever so many questions about two men that came here last Friday night.'

'Oh yes,' said Fatty, at once. 'I know the men—actors, aren't they? I've got their autographs in my autograph album. Were they here on Friday, then? I bet they liked your snacks.'

'Yes, they came on Friday,' said the little girl. 'I know, because it was my birthday, and Peter Watting brought me a book. I'd just been listening to Radio Fun at half-past six, when they came in.'

'Half-past six,' said Fatty. 'Well, what did they do then? Eat all your snacks?'

'No! They only have coffee and sandwiches,' said the little girl. 'They gave me the book—it's a beauty, I'll show you—and then we listened to Radio Theatre at seven o'clock. And then something went wrong with the wireless and it stopped.'

'Oh,' said Fatty, disappointed, because he had been counting on the wireless for checking up on the time. 'What happened then?'

'Well, Peter Watting's very good with wirelesses,' said the little girl. 'So he said he'd try and mend it. Mother said, "Mend it in time for eight o'clock then, because I want to hear a concert then."'

'And was it mended by then?' asked Fatty.

'I'M FED UP WITH YOU KIDS!'

'No. Not till twenty past eight,' said the little girl. 'Mother was very disappointed. But we got it going by then, quite all right—twenty past eight, I mean—and then Peter and William had to go. They called the ferry and went across the river.'

This was all very interesting. It certainly proved beyond a doubt that William Orr and Peter Watting could not possibly have had anything to do with the robbery at the Little Theatre. That was certain. The little girl was quite obviously telling the truth.

'Well, thanks for a jolly good meal,' said Fatty. 'How much do we owe you?'

The little girl gave a squeal. 'Oh, I never counted your snacks. Do you know how many you had? I shan't half catch it from Mother if she knows I didn't count.'

'Well, you ought to count,' said Fatty. 'It's too much like hard work for us to count when we're eating. Larry, I make it six snacks each, the sandwiches and the coffee. Is that correct?'

It was. Fatty paid up, gave the little girl a shilling to buy herself something for the birthday she had had on Friday, and went off with Larry, feeling decidedly full.

'We've just got time to go to the cinema to see if we can pick up anything about John James' visit,' said Fatty. 'Oh dear—I wish I hadn't snacked quite so much. I don't feel very brainy at the moment.'

They went into the little lobby. There was a girl at a table, marking off piles of tickets.

'Good morning,' said Fatty. 'Er—could you tell us anything about last week's programme?'

'Why? Are you thinking of going to it?' said the girl, with a giggle. 'You're a bit late.'

'My friend and I have been having a bit of an argument about it,' said Fatty, making this up on the spur of the moment, whilst Larry looked at him in surprise. 'You see, my friend thinks the programme was *The Yearling* and I said it was—er—er —*Henry V*.'

'No, no,' said the girl, graciously. 'It was *The Weakling*, not *The Yearling*, and *Henry the Fifteenth*, not *Henry V*.'

Fatty turned crossly and went out. He bumped into somebody coming up the steps.

He nearly fell, and clutched hold of the person he had collided with. A familiar voice grated on his ear.

'Take your hands off me! Wherever I go I find one of you kids! What you doing *here*, I'd like to know?'

'They wanted to take tickets for last week's programme,' called the girl from inside, and screamed with laughter. 'Cheek! I told them off all right.'

'That's right,' said Mr. Goon. 'They want telling off. Coming and bothering you with silly questions.' Then it suddenly struck him that Fatty was coming about the same thing as he was— to check up on an alibi. He swung round in a rage. 'Poking your N . . .' he began.

But Fatty had gone, and so had Larry. They were not going to stay and argue with Mr. Goon and That Girl.

'Cheek,' said Fatty, who was not easily out done in any conversation. 'I'm afraid Goon will get a lot more out of her than we shall.'

'Yes. We've rather fallen down on this alibi,' said Larry—and then he stopped and gave Fatty a sudden punch. 'I say—I know! We can ask Kitty, Pip's cook. She goes to the pictures every single Friday. She told Bets so one day and I heard her. She said she'd never missed for nine years.'

'Well, I bet she missed last Friday, for the first time then,' said Fatty, gloomily. The cinema girl's cheek was still rankling. 'Anyway, we'll ask and see.'

'Well, thank goodness we're not likely to run into Goon in Pip's kitchen,' said Larry.

They arrived at Pip's, and went into the kitchen. Kitty beamed at them, especially at Fatty, whom she thought very clever indeed.

'Kitty, could we possibly have a drink of water?' began Fatty.

'You shall have some home-made lemonade,' said Kitty. 'And would you like a snack to go with it?'

The very idea of a snack made Fatty turn pale. 'No, thanks awfully,' he said. 'I've just had a snack, Kitty.'

'Well, do have another,' said Kitty, and brought out some small and very tempting-looking sausage-rolls. Fatty groaned and turned away.

'Sorry, Kitty—they look marvellous—but I'm too full of snacks to risk another.'

There was a pause whilst Kitty filled lemonade-glasses.

'Did you go to the pictures last week?' said Larry. 'You always do, don't you?'

'Never missed for nine years,' said Kitty proudly. 'Yes, I went on Friday, same as usual. Oooh, it was a *lovely* picture.'

'What was it ?' asked Fatty.

'Well, I went in at six and the news was on,' said Kitty. 'Then a cartoon, you know. Made me laugh like anything. Then at half-past six till the end of the programme there was *He Loved Her So*. Oooh, it was *lovely*. Made me cry ever so.'

'A really happy evening,' said Fatty. 'See any one you know ?'

Kitty considered. 'No, I don't know as I did. I always get kind of wrapped up in the picture, you know. It was a pity it broke down.'

Fatty pricked up his ears. 'What do you mean —broke down ?'

'Well, you know what I mean, Master Frederick,' said Kitty. 'The picture sort of snaps—and stops —and there's only the screen, and no picture. I suppose the film breaks or something.'

'Did it do that a lot ?' asked Fatty.

'Yes—four times,' said Kitty. 'All the way through, it seemed. Just at the wrong bits too —you know, the real exciting bits ! Every one was grumbling about it.'

'Pity,' said Fatty, getting up. 'Well, Kitty, thanks awfully for the lemonade—and I hope you enjoy your picture *this* Friday.'

'Oooh I shall,' said Kitty. 'It's called *Three Broken Hearts*.'

'You'll weep like anything,' said Fatty. 'You *will* enjoy that, Kitty. It's a pity I'll be too busy to come and lend you my hanky.'

'Oh, you are a caution,' said Kitty, delighted.

'Come on, Larry,' said Fatty, and he pulled him out of Kitty's kitchen. 'We've learnt something there ! Now, if we can only get hold of John James

and find out if *he* noticed the breaks in the picture—
which he must have done if he was there—we shall
be able to check *his* alibi all right ! '

' So we shall,' said Larry. ' Jolly good work.
But how can we get hold of John James ? We can't
just walk up to him and say, " Did you notice the
breaks in the picture, Mr. James, when you were at
the cinema on Friday ? " '

' Of course we can't,' said Fatty. ' Gosh, it's
almost dinner-time. We'll have to do that afterwards,
Larry. Can you possibly eat any dinner ? I can't.'

' No, I can't—and it's hot roast pork and apple
sauce to-day,' said Larry with a groan. ' What a
waste.'

' Don't even *mention* roast pork,' said Fatty with
a shudder. ' Why did we eat so many snacks ?
Now my mother's going to worry because I can't
eat a thing at dinner to-day—take my temperature
or something ! '

' What about John James ? ' said Larry. ' How
are we going to tackle him ? We don't even know
where to find him. He won't be at the theatre
because there's no show this afternoon.'

' I'll ring up Zoe when I get home and see if
she knows where we can get hold of him,' said
Fatty. ' We'd better take Bets too. She'll be feeling
left out if we don't.'

' Right,' said Larry. ' See you this afternoon
sometime.'

XIX. JOHN JAMES AND THE CINEMA

VERY fortunately for Fatty his mother was not in to lunch, so he was able to eat as little as he liked without any one noticing. He was only at the table about five minutes and then he went to ring up Zoe, hoping she was at her sister's as usual.

She was. 'Oh—hallo, Zoe,' said Fatty. 'I say, can you tell me something ? I want to have a talk with John James, if I can. Do you know if he'll be anywhere about this afternoon ? '

'Well—let me see,' said Zoe's clear voice over the telephone. 'I did hear him say something about going across the river in the ferry, and taking a picnic-tea up on the hill beyond. There's a marvellous view up there, you know.'

'Yes. I know,' said Fatty. 'Oh, good—I'll slip across and see if I can spot him there. Do you know what time he is going ? '

Zoe didn't know. Then she told Fatty that Mr. Goon was going to see poor Boysie again that evening. 'And I heard him say that he's not going to stand any nonsense this time—Boysie's got to "come clean," the horrid fellow,' said Zoe, indignantly. 'As if he can make Boysie confess to something he doesn't know anything about ! '

Fatty frowned as he hung up the receiver. He was afraid that Boysie *might* confess to the robbery, out of sheer terror and desperation. What a dreadful thing that would be—to have him confess to something he hadn't done—and have the real culprit go scot-free.

Fatty rang up Larry, and then Pip, telling them of John James' plans for the afternoon. 'We've got to go and check up on his alibi,' he said. 'And we can only do that by questioning *him*—to see if he really was at the cinema on Friday night. And as it's a smashing day, let's all take our tea and go for a picnic up on the hill across the river, and kill two birds with one stone—enjoy ourselves, and do a spot of detecting as well!'

The others thought this was a splendid idea. 'Fatty always thinks of such nice things,' said Bets, happily. 'It will be lovely up there on the hills.'

Fatty had told Pip to go and ask Kitty once more about the breaks in the picture on Friday night, just to make sure he had got it quite right. 'Ask if she remembers *exactly* how many breaks there were, when they came—and, if possible, the *time*,' said Fatty. 'Write it down, Pip, in case you forget the details. This may be important. It looks as if John James is our only hope now— I feel that we must count Alec Grant out, with his alibi of over a hundred people.'

The children met at the ferry at a quarter to three, laden with picnic-bags. Pip carried a mackintosh-rug. 'Mother made me,' he said, crossly. 'She said the grass is still damp. You're lucky to have a mother that doesn't fuss about things like that.'

'Mine fusses about other things,' said Fatty. 'And Larry's fusses about certain things too. Never mind, it's not much bother to sit down on a rug!'

'As a matter of fact,' said Bets, seriously, 'I've met one or two mothers who never never fussed about their children—but, you know, I'm sure it

was because they didn't care tuppence about them.
I think I'd rather have a fussy mother, really.'

'Here's the boat,' said Fatty, as the ferryman
came rowing across. 'I'll pay for every one. It's
only tuppence each.'

They got into the boat. 'Rowed any one across
yet this afternoon?' asked Fatty. The boatman
shook his head. 'No, not yet. Bit early.'

'Then John James hasn't gone across yet,'
said Fatty to the others. 'Hey, Buster—don't
take a header into the water, will you?'

They got across and made their way over a
field and up a steep hill to the top. Fatty chose
a place from where they could see the ferry.

'We'll watch and see when the ferryman goes
out,' he said. 'I don't know if we could make
out John James from here, but I expect we could.
He's so burly.'

The spring sun was hot. The cowslips around
nodded their yellow heads in the breeze. It was
very pleasant up there on the hill. Larry yawned
and lay down.

'You watch for J. J., you others,' he said. 'I'm
going to have a nap!'

But he hadn't been asleep for more than ten
minutes when Fatty prodded him in the middle.
'Wake up, Larry. Can you see if that's John James
standing on the opposite side of the river, waiting
for the ferry?'

Larry sat up. He had very keen eyes. He
screwed them up and looked hard. 'Yes. I think
it is,' he said. 'Let's hope he comes this way. I
don't feel like walking miles after him.'

Fortunately it *was* John James, and he *did*

come that way. The children watched him get into the boat, lnad on their side of the river, and follow the same path as they had taken themselves.

'Now,' said Fatty, getting up, 'we'd better start wandering about till we see where he's going to sit. Then we'll settle somewhere near.'

'How are we going to start the checking up?' asked Pip.

'I'll start it,' said Fatty. 'And then you can all follow my lead, and ask innocent questions. Roll up your rug, Pip.'

The five children and Buster wandered about and picked cowslips, keeping a sharp eye on John James, who was coming very slowly up the hill. He found a sheltered place with a bush behind him, and lay down at full length, his arms behind his head so that he might look down the hill towards the river.

Fatty wandered near him. 'Here's a good place,' he called to the others. 'We'll have the rug here.' Then he turned politely to the man near by.

'I hope we shan't disturb you if we sit just here,' he said.

'Not if you don't yell and screech,' said John James. 'But I don't suppose you will. You look as if you'd all been well brought up!'

'I hope we have,' said Fatty, and beckoned to the others. Pip put down the rug. By this time the man was sitting up, and had put a cigarette in his mouth. He patted himself all over and frowned.

'I suppose,' he said to Fatty, 'I suppose you

haven't got matches on you, by any chance ?   I've left mine at home.'

Fatty always had every conceivable thing on him, on the principle that you simply never knew what you might want at any time.   He presented John James with a full box of matches at once.

'Keep the whole box,' said Fatty.   'I'm not smoking till I'm twenty-one ! '

'Good boy,' said John James.   'Very sensible. Thanks, old chap.   I say—haven't I seen you before ? '

'Yes,' said Fatty.   'We came into the back of the theatre yesterday—and you were good enough to sign our autograph albums.'

'Oh yes—now I remember you all,' said John James.   'Have you come up here for a picnic ? '

'Yes.   We're just about to begin,' said Fatty, though it was really much too early.   But the effect of the snacks was beginning to wear off, and the lack of a midday meal was making itself felt !   Fatty was more than ready for a picnic.   'Er—I suppose you wouldn't join us, sir—we've got plenty.'

'Yes, I will,' said John James.   'I've got some stuff here too.   We'll pool it.'

It was a very nice picnic, with plenty to eat, and some of Kitty's home-made lemonade to drink. For a short while Fatty and the others talked about whatever came into their heads.

Then Fatty began his ' checking.'   'What's on at the cinema this week, Larry ? ' he asked.

Larry told him.   'Oh no,' said Fatty, ' that was last week ! '

'You're wrong,' said John James at once. ' It was *Here Goes*, the first part of the week, and

11

He Loved Her So, the second. Both absolutely frightful.'

'Really?' said Fatty. 'I heard that *He Loved Her So* was good. But I didn't see it. I suppose you did?'

'Yes. Saw it on Friday,' said John James. 'At least—I *would* have seen it, but it was so boring that I fell asleep nearly all the time!'

This remark disappointed all the Find-Outers very much indeed. If John James slept all the time, he wouldn't have noticed the breaks in the picture—and so they wouldn't be able to check his alibi.

'Hope you didn't snore!' said Fatty. 'But I suppose people would wake you up if you did.'

'I did keep waking up,' said John James. 'I kept on waking because of people talking and sounding annoyed. I don't quite know what happened—I think the picture must have broken unexpectedly—like they do sometimes, you know—and that made the audience fidgety and cross. But I soon went to sleep again.'

'Bad luck, to be woken up like that!' laughed Fatty. 'I hope you didn't get disturbed from your nap *too* many times!'

John James considered. 'Well, I should think that wretched picture must have gone wrong at least four times,' he said. 'I remember looking at the clock once or twice—once I got woken up at quarter to seven, and another time at ten past. I remember wondering where on earth I was when I woke up then. Thought I was in bed at home!'

'Bit of a boring evening for you,' said Fatty, watching Pip take out his note-book and do a bit of checking up on times. He nodded reassuringly to Fatty. Yes, John James' alibi was safe all right. There was no doubt at all that he had been in the cinema that evening, and had been awakened each time the picture broke, by the noise of the impatient people around.

'Yes. It was boring,' said John James. 'But it was something to do. Help yourself to my cherry cake. Do. There's plenty.'

The talk turned to the robbery at the theatre.

'Who do *you* think did it?' asked Fatty.

'I haven't a notion,' said John James. 'Not a notion. Boysie didn't. I'm sure of that. He hasn't the brains or the pluck for a thing of that sort. He's a harmless sort of fellow. He just adores Zoe—and I'm not surprised. She's sweet to him.'

They talked for a little while longer and then Fatty got up and shook the crumbs off himself. 'Well, thanks for letting us picnic with you, Mr. James,' he said. 'We'll have to be going now. Are you coming too?'

'No. I'll sit here a bit longer,' said John James. 'There's going to be a grand sunset later on.'

The Find-Outers went down the hill, with Buster capering along on his short legs. 'Well,' said Fatty, when they were out of hearing, 'John James is out of our list of Suspects. His alibi is first-rate. He was in the cinema all right on Friday evening. Gosh, this mystery really is getting deeper and deeper. I'm stumped!'

'Oh *no*, Fatty!' said Bets, quite shocked to hear Fatty say this. 'You *can't* be stumped! Not with your wonderful brains!'

XX. DEFEAT—AND A BRAINWAVE

FATTY racked his brains that night, but to no effect. However much he thought and thought, he could see no solution to the mystery at all. He was certain Boysie hadn't done the job. He was also quite certain that Zoe, whose alibi was a little shaky, had had nothing to do with it either. Every one else had unshakable alibis. It was true they hadn't checked Alec Grant's, but Fatty had looked up a local paper and had seen a report of the one-man concert that Alec had given on the Friday evening at Sheepridge.

'The report in the paper is a good enough alibi,' he said to the others. 'We needn't bother any more about Alec. But WHO is the culprit? Who did the job?'

In desperation he went down that evening to talk to P.C. Pippin. He was there, walking up and down Goon's little back garden, smoking a pipe. He was pleased to see Fatty.

'Any news?' said Fatty. 'I suppose Goon's out?'

'Yes, thank goodness,' said Pippin, feelingly. 'He's been at me all day long about something or other. Pops in and out on that bike of his, and doesn't give me any peace at all. He's gone down to see Boysie again now. I'm very much afraid he'll scare him into a false confession.'

'Yes. I'm afraid of that too,' said Fatty. 'What about Zoe? Does Goon think she had anything to do with it?'

'I'm afraid he does,' said Pippin. 'He's got that handkerchief of hers with Z on, you know— that's one of his main pieces of evidence.'

'But that's nonsense!' said Fatty. 'The hand-kerchief might have been on that verandah for days! It doesn't prove she was there that night.'

'Goon thinks it does,' said Pippin. 'You see, he has found out that the cleaner swept that verandah clean on Friday afternoon at four o'clock! So the hanky must have been dropped after that.'

Fatty bit his lip and frowned. That was very bad indeed. He hadn't known that. Of *course* Goon thought Zoe had crept to that verandah that evening and been let in by Boysie, if he found a hanky there with Z on—a hanky which must have been dropped after four o'clock! That was a very nasty bit of evidence indeed.

'What annoys Goon is that Zoe keeps on denying it's her hanky,' said Pippin. 'Says she's never seen it before. It's a pity it's got Z on—such an unusual initial.'

'I know,' groaned poor Fatty, feeling very much inclined to make a clean breast of how he had planted the handkerchief and all the other 'clues' on the verandah himself. Well—if Goon did arrest Zoe and Boysie, he would certainly *have* to own up. He turned to Pippin.

'Telephone me, Pippin, if you hear any serious news—such as Goon getting a false confession from Boysie—or making an arrest,' he said.

Pippin nodded. 'I certainly will. What have *you* been doing about the mystery? I bet you haven't been idle!'

Fatty told him how he had checked up all

the alibis and found them unshakable—except for Zoe's. He was feeling very worried indeed. It would be awful if Goon solved the mystery the wrong way—and got the wrong persons! If only, only Fatty could see a bit of daylight. But he couldn't.

He went back home, quite depressed, which was very unusual for Fatty. Larry telephoned him that evening to find out if he had heard anything fresh from Pippin.

Fatty told him all he knew. Larry listened in silence.

' Well—what are we going to do next ? ' he asked.

For once Fatty was completely at a loss. There didn't seem anything to do at all. ' I don't see *what* we can do,' he said, miserably. ' I'm absolutely stuck. Fat lot of good we are at detecting ! We'll have to break up the Find-Outers Band if we can't do better than this.'

' Come up at ten to-morrow and have a meeting,' said Larry. ' We'll all think hard and talk and go over absolutely *every*thing. There's something we've missed, I'm sure—some idea we haven't thought of. There's no mystery without a solution, Fatty. Cheer up. We'll find it ! '

But before ten o'clock the next day came, the telephone rang, and Pippin relayed some very bad news to Fatty.

' Are you there ? I've only got a minute. Mr. Goon has got a confession from Boysie ! And Zoe's in it too ! Apparently Boysie said he and Zoe worked the thing together. He let Zoe in at the verandah door, they made the tea, Boysie took the

cup up with the dope in to the manager—then when
he fell asleep, Zoe went up and robbed the safe.
She apparently knew where the key was and everything.'

Fatty listened in horror. ' But, Pippin ! *Pippin !*
Boysie couldn't have done it—nor could Zoe. Goon's
forced that confession out of a poor fellow who's so
queer in his head he doesn't really know what he's
saying.'

There was a pause. ' Well, I'm inclined to agree
with you,' said Pippin. ' In fact—well, I shouldn't
tell you this, but I must—I think from what Goon
has let slip, he *did* force that false confession from
Boysie, poor wretch. Now, see here, I'm helpless.
I can't go against Goon. You're the only one that
can do anything. Isn't Inspector Jenks a *great*
friend of yours ? Won't he believe what you
say, if you tell him you think there's been a
mistake ? '

' But I haven't any *proof*,' wailed Fatty. ' Now,
if I *knew* who the robber was, and could produce
him, with real evidence, the Inspector would listen
to me like a shot. I'll go and see the others, and see
what they think. If we can't think of anything
better, I'll cycle over to the next town and see the
Inspector myself.'

' Well, you'd better make . . .' began Pippin,
and then Fatty heard the receiver being put back
with a click. He guessed that Goon had come in.
He sat by the telephone and thought hard. This
was frightful. Poor Zoe. Poor Boysie. What in
the world could he do to help them ?

He tore off to Pip's on his bicycle. The others
were there already. They looked gloomy—and they

looked gloomier still when Fatty told them what Pippin had said.

'It's serious,' said Larry. 'More serious than any other mystery we've tackled. What can we do, Fatty?'

'We'll go through all the Suspects and the Alibis, and run through all we know,' said Fatty, getting out his note-book. 'I've got everything down here. Listen whilst I read it—and think, think, think *hard* all the time. As Larry says—we've missed something—some clue, or some evidence that would help us. There's something very wrong, and probably the explanation is sticking out a mile —if we could only *see* it!'

He began to read through his notes—the list of Suspects. The alibis they had each given. The checking of all the alibis. Boysie's account of the evening of the crime. The manager's own account. The dislike that each member of the show felt for the manager, which would give each one of them a motive for paying him out. Everything in his note-book Fatty read out, clearly and slowly, and the Find-Outers listened intently, even Buster sitting still with ears cocked.

He finished. There was a long pause. Fatty looked up. 'Any suggestions?' he asked, not very hopefully.

The others shook their heads. Fatty shut his note-book with a snap. 'Defeated!' he said, bitterly. 'Beaten! All we know is that out of the seven people who are Suspects, the two who *could* have done it, didn't—Boysie and Zoe—we *know* they didn't. They're incapable of doing such a thing. And the others, who *might* have done it, all have

first-class alibis. How *can* the Pantomime Cat
have done the deed when it isn't in his nature to
do it ? '

'It almost makes you think it must have been
somebody else in Boysie's skin,' said Bets.

The others laughed scornfully, 'Silly!' said
Pip, and Bets went red.

And then Fatty went suddenly and inexplicably
mad. He stared at Bets with fixed and glassy eyes.
Then he smacked her hard on the shoulder. Then
he got up and did a solemn and ridiculous dance
round the room, looking as if he was in the seventh
heaven of delight.

'Bets!' he said, stopping at last. '*Bets!* Good,
clever, brainy old Bets. She's got it! She's solved
it! Bets, you deserve to be head of the Find-Outers!
Oh my word, Bets, why, why, why didn't I think of
it before ? '

The others all stared at him as if he was out of
his mind. 'Fatty, don't be an ass. Tell us what
you mean,' said Pip, crossly. 'What's Bets been so
clever about ? For the life of me I don't know! '

'Nor do I,' said Larry. 'Sit down, Fatty, and
explain.'

Fatty sat down, beaming all over his face. He
put his arm round the astonished Bets and squeezed
her. 'Dear old Bets—she's saved Boysie and Zoe.
What brains! '

'*Fatty!* Shut up and tell us what you mean! '
almost yelled Pip in exasperation.

'Right,' said Fatty. 'You heard what young
Bets said, didn't you ? She said, " It almost makes
you think it must have been somebody else in Boysie's
skin." Well ? Well, I ask you ? Can't you see

that's the solution ? Turnip-heads, you don't see it yet ! '

' I'm beginning to see,' said Larry, slowly. ' But you see it *all*, Fatty, obviously. Tell us.'

' Now, look here,' said Fatty. ' Boysie says he did *not* take the tea in to the manager, doesn't he ? But the manager swears he *did*. And why does he swear that ? Because Boysie, he says, was wearing his cat-skin. All right. Whoever brought the tea was certainly the Pantomime Cat—but as the manager never saw who was *inside* the skin, how does he know it was Boysie ? '

The others listened in amazement.

' And as it happens, it *wasn't* Boysie ! ' said Fatty, triumphantly. ' Let me tell you what *I* think happened that night, now that Bets has opened my eyes.'

' Yes, go on, tell us,' said Pip, getting excited as he too began to see what Fatty was getting at.

' Well—the theatre cast all departed, as we know, at half-past five, because we saw them go,' said Fatty. ' Only Boysie was left, because he lives there, and the manager was upstairs in his office.

' Now, there was a member of the cast who had a grudge against the manager, and wanted to pay him out. So that night, after *we* had gone home from our planting of false clues, this person came silently back—let himself in secretly, because Boysie didn't see him or he would have said so—and hid till he saw Boysie making the tea. He knew that Boysie always made tea and took a cup to the manager.

' Very well. Boysie made the tea, and poured himself out a cup. But he didn't drink it because it was too hot. He waited till it was cooler. And the hidden person slipped out, and put a sleeping-draught into Boysie's cup.

'Boysie drank it, felt terribly sleepy, went into the verandah room and snored by the fire. The hidden person then made sure that Boysie was doped and wouldn't wake up—and he *stripped the skin off Boysie* . . .'

'And put it on himself!' cried all the others together. 'Oh, *Fatty*!'

'Yes—he put it on himself. And made a cup of tea for the manager, putting into it a sleeping-draught of course—and up the stairs he went! Well, how could the manager guess it was any one but Boysie in his Pantomime Cat-skin! Wouldn't *any* one think that?'

'Of course,' said Daisy. 'And then he waited till the manager had drunk his tea and fallen asleep —and did the robbery!'

'Exactly,' said Fatty. 'Took down the mirror, found the key in the manager's wallet, worked out the combination that would open the safe—and stole everything in it. Then he went down to the sleeping Boysie and pulled him into the skin again —and departed as secretly as he came, with the money!

'He knew that when the cup of tea was examined and traces of a sleeping-draught were found, the first question asked would be—*Who* brought up the cup of tea to the manager?' said Fatty. 'And the answer to that—quite untruly as it happens—was, of course, Boysie.'

'Oh, Fatty—it's wonderful,' said Bets, her face shining. 'We've solved the mystery!'

'We haven't,' said Larry and Pip together.

'We *have*,' said Bets indignantly.

'Ah, wait a minute, Bets,' said Fatty. 'We know how the thing was done—but the *real* mystery now is—*who was inside the skin of the Pantomime Cat?*'

XXI. THE LAST ALIBI IS CHECKED

EVERY one felt tremendously excited. Larry smacked Bets proudly on the back. 'You just hit the nail on the head, Bets, when you made that brainy remark of yours,' he said.

'Well—I didn't know it was brainy,' said Bets. 'I just said it without thinking, really.'

'I *told* you there was something sticking out a mile, right under our very noses,' said Fatty. 'And that was it. Come on, now—we've got to find out who was in the skin.'

They all thought. 'But what's the good of thinking it's this person or that person?' said Pip at last. 'If we say "John James," for instance, it can't be, because we've checked his alibi and it's perfect.'

'Let's not worry about alibis,' said Fatty. 'Once we decide who the person was, inside the cat-skin, we'll re-check the alibi—and what's more, we'll then find it's false! It must be. Come on, now—who was inside that cat-skin?'

'Not John James,' said Daisy. 'He was much too big—too fat.'

'Yes—it would have to be a small person,' said Fatty. 'Boysie is small, and only a person about his size could wear that skin.'

They all ran their minds over the members of the cast. Larry thumped on the floor.

'Alec Grant! He's the smallest of the lot—very neat and dapper and slim—don't you remember?'

'Yes! The others are *all* too big—even the two girls, who are too tall to fit the skin,' said Fatty. 'Alec Grant is the only member who could possibly get into the skin.'

'*And* he split it!' said Daisy, suddenly. 'Oh, don't you remember, Fatty, how Boysie came and asked Zoe to mend it for him—and she looked at the splitting seams and said he must be getting fat? Well, he wasn't! Somebody bigger than he was had used his skin and split it!'

'Gosh, yes,' said Fatty. 'Would you believe it —a Clue as big as that staring us in the face and we never noticed it! But I say—*Alec Grant!* He's got the best alibi of the whole lot.'

'He certainly has,' said Larry. 'It's going to be a hard alibi to break, too. Impossible, it seems to me.'

'No. Not impossible,' said Fatty. 'He couldn't be in two places at once. And so, if he was in the Pantomime Cat's skin at the Little Theatre on Friday evening, he was *not* giving a concert at Sheepridge! That's certain.'

'Fancy! The only alibi we didn't check,' said Larry.

'Yes—and I *said* that a good detective always checks everything, whether he thinks it is necessary or not,' groaned Fatty. 'I must be going downhill rapidly. I consider I've done very badly over this!'

'You haven't, Fatty,' said Bets. 'Why, it was you who saw that my remark, which was really only a joke, was the real clue to the mystery! I didn't see that, and nor did the others.'

'How are we going to shake this alibi of Alec

Grant's ? ' said Larry. ' Let's keep to the subject. We haven't much time, it seems to me, if Goon has got a false confession from poor Boysie. He'll be getting into touch with the Inspector any time now and making an arrest—two arrests, I suppose, if Zoe has to be in it too.'

' Any one got friends in Sheepridge ? ' asked Fatty, suddenly.

' I've got a cousin there—you know him, Freddie Wilson,' said Larry. ' Why ? '

' Well, I suppose there's a chance he might have gone to Alec's concert,' said Fatty. ' Telephone him and see, Larry. We've got to find out something about this concert now.'

' *Freddie* won't have gone to a concert like that —to see a man impersonating women,' said Larry, scornfully.

' You go and phone him,' said Fatty. ' Ask him if he knows anything about it.'

Larry went, rather reluctantly. He was afraid that Freddie would jeer at his enquiry.

But Freddie was out and it was his eighteen-year-old sister, Julia, who answered. And she provided an enormous bit of luck !

' No, Larry, Freddie didn't go,' she said. ' *Can* you see him going to *any* kind of concert ? I can't. But I went with Mother. Alec Grant was awfully good—honestly, you couldn't have told he was a man. I waited afterwards and got his autograph.'

' Hold on a minute,' said Larry, and went to report to Fatty. Fatty leapt up as if he had been shot. ' Got his *autograph* ! Gosh—this is super. Don't you remember, idiot, *we've* all got his autograph too ! I'd like to see the autograph *Julia* got ! I'll eat my hat if it isn't quite different from the ones *we've* got ! '

' But Fatty—Alec Grant was there, giving the concert,' began Larry. ' Julia says so.'

Fatty took absolutely no notice of him but rushed to the telephone, with Buster excitedly at his heels, feeling that there really must be Something Up !

' Julia ! Frederick Trotteville here. I say, *could* I come over and see you by the next bus ? Most important. Will you be in ? '

Julia laughed at Fatty's urgent voice. ' Oh, Frederick—you sound as if you're in the middle of a mystery or something. Yes, of course. Come over. I'll be most interested to know what you want ! '

Fatty clicked down the receiver and rushed back to the others. ' I'm off to Sheepridge,' he said. ' Coming, any one ? '

' Of *course*,' said every one at once. What ! Be left out just when things were getting so thrilling ! No, every one was determined to be in at the death.

They arrived at Sheepridge an hour later, and went to find Julia. She was waiting for them, and was amused to see the whole five march in.

' Listen, Julia,' began Fatty. ' I can't explain everything to you now—it would take too long— but we are very curious about Alec Grant. You say he really was there, performing at the concert ? You actually recognized him, and have seen him before ? '

' Yes. Of course I recognized him,' said Julia.

Fatty felt a little taken-aback. He had hoped Julia would say she didn't recognize him, and then he might be able to prove that somebody else had taken Alec's place.

'Have you your autograph - album with his signature in?' he asked. Julia went to get it. All the Find-Outers had brought theirs with them, and Fatty silently compared the five signatures in their books with the one in Julia's.

Julia's was utterly and entirely different!

'Look,' said Fatty, pointing. 'The autographs he did for us are illegible squiggles—the one he did for Julia is perfectly clear and readable. It *wasn't* Alec Grant who did that!'

'You'll be saying it was his twin-sister next,' said Julia with a laugh.

Fatty stared as if he couldn't believe his ears. 'What did you say?' he almost shouted. '*Twin-sister!* Julia—you don't really mean to say he's got a twin-sister?'

'Of course he has,' said Julia. 'What *is* all this mystery about? I've seen his sister—exactly like him, small and neat: She doesn't live here, she lives at Marlow.'

Fatty let out an enormous sigh. 'Why didn't I think of a twin?' he said. 'Of course! The *only* solution! He got his twin to come and do his show for him. Is she good too, Julia?'

'Well, they're both in shows,' said Julia. 'As a matter of fact, Alec is supposed to be much better than Nora, his sister. I thought he wasn't so good last Friday, really—he had such a terrible cold, for one thing, and kept stopping to cough.'

The others immediately looked at one another.

12

Oho! A cough and a cold! Certainly Alec hadn't had one on Monday afternoon when they had all heard him sing. Nobody had seen any sign of a cold or cough then. Very, very suspicious!

'May we take this album away for a little while?' asked Fatty. 'I'll send it back. Thanks so much for seeing us. You've been a great help.'

'I don't know how,' said Julia. 'It seems very mysterious to me.'

'It *has* been very mysterious,' said Fatty, preparing to go. 'Very, very mysterious. But I see daylight now, though I very—nearly—didn't!'

The Five Find-Outers went off with Buster, excited and talkative. 'We've got it all straightened out now,' said Fatty, happily. 'Thanks to Bets. Honestly, Bets, we'd have been absolutely stumped if you hadn't made that sudden remark. It was a brainwave.'

They got back to Peterswood, having decided what to do. They would go and see Pippin first, and tell him all they knew. Fatty said they owed it to him to do that, and if he wanted to arrest Alec Grant, he could. What sucks for Goon!

But when they got to Goon's house, they had a shock. Pippin was there alone, looking very gloomy.

'Ah, Master Frederick,' he said, when he saw Fatty, 'I've been trying to telephone you for the last hour. Mr. Goon's arrested Boysie and Zoe, and they're both in an awful state! I'm afraid Boysie will go right off his head now.'

'Where are they?' asked Fatty, desperately.

'Goon's taken them over to the Inspector,'

'MR. GOON'S ARRESTED BOYSIE AND ZOE, AND THEY'RE BOTH
IN AN AWFUL STATE!'

said Pippin. 'What's the matter with *you*? You look all of a dither.'

'I am,' said Fatty, sitting down suddenly. 'Pippin, listen hard to what I'm going to tell you. And then tell us what to do. Prepare for some shocks. Now—listen!'

XXII. A SURPRISE FOR THE INSPECTOR!

PIPPIN listened, his eyes almost falling out of his head. He heard about the false clues and frowned. He heard about the way the children had interviewed the Suspects by means of asking for autographs— he heard about the tea-party—the checking up of the alibis—and then he heard of Bets' bright remark that had suddenly set Fatty on the right track.

The autograph albums were produced and compared. The visit to Sheepridge related. The twin-sister came into the story, and P.C. Pippin rubbed his forehead in bewilderment as Fatty produced the many, many pieces of the jigsaw puzzle that, all fitted together, made up a clear solution of the mystery.

'Well! I don't know what to think,' said poor Pippin. 'This beats me! Goon's got the wrong ones, no doubt about that. And I think there's no doubt that Alec Grant is the culprit.'

'Can you arrest him then and take him to the Inspector?' cried Fatty.

'No. Of course not,' said Pippin. 'Not just on what you've told me. But I'll tell you what we *can* do—I can go and get him for questioning. I can take him over to the Inspector and face him with all you've said.'

'Oh *yes*—that's a fine idea,' said Fatty. 'Can we come too?'

'You'll have to,' said Pippin. 'My word, I shan't like to look at the Inspector's face when he hears about those false clues of yours. Good thing you've solved the mystery, that's all I can say. Let's hope that will cancel out the mischief you got into first.'

Pippin's voice was stern, but his eyes twinkled. ' Can't be really cross with you myself,' he said. ' Your clues put me where I could see the crime when it was just done—and now it looks as if I'll be able to show Goon up. He deserves it, browbeating that poor, queer-headed fellow into a false confession ! '

The morning went on being more and more exciting. Alec Grant was collected from the theatre, where he was rehearsing with the others, who were most alarmed at Zoe's arrest. He put on a very bold face and pretended that he hadn't the least idea why Pippin wanted to question him.

He was very surprised to see all the children also crammed into the big car that Pippin had hired to take them over to see the Inspector. But nobody explained anything to him. The children looked away from him. Horrid, beastly thief—and how *could* he let Zoe and Boysie take the blame for something he himself had done ?

Pippin telephoned to the Inspector before they left. ' Sir ? Pippin here. About that Little Theatre job. I believe Mr. Goon's brought his two arrests over to you. Well, sir, can you hold things up for a bit ? I've got some fresh evidence here, sir. Very important. I'm bringing some one over to question —man named Alec Grant. Also, sir, I'm bringing —er—five children.'

' *What ?* ' said Inspector Jenks, thinking he must have misheard. ' Five *what* ? '

' CHILDREN, sir,' said Pippin. ' You know, sir,

you told me about them before I came here. One's
a boy called Frederick Trotteville.'

'Oh, *really* ? ' said the Inspector. 'That's most
interesting. So he's been working on this too, has
he ? Do you know what conclusions he has come to,
Pippin ? '

'Yes, sir, I know all about it,' said Pippin.
'Er—Mr. Goon didn't want me to work with him
on this case, sir, so—er—well . . .'

'So you worked with Frederick, I suppose,'
said the Inspector. 'Very wise of you. Well—I'll
hold things up till you come.'

He called Goon into his room. 'Er, Goon,'
he said, 'we must wait for about twenty minutes
before proceeding with anything. Pippin has just
phoned through. He's got fresh evidence.'

Goon bristled like a hedgehog. '*Pippin*, sir ?
He doesn't know a thing about this case. Not a
thing. I wouldn't let him work with me on it, he's
such a turnip-head. Course, he's only been with me
a little while, but it's easy to see he's not going to be
much good. Not enough brains. And a bit too
cocky, sir, if you'll excuse the slang.'

'Certainly,' said the Inspector. 'Well, we will
wait. Pippin is bringing a man for questioning.'

Goon's mouth fell open. 'A man—for questioning ? But we've *got* the people who did the job now.
What's he want to bring a man for ? Who is it ? '

'And he's also bringing five children, he says,'
went on the Inspector, enjoying himself very much,
for he did not like the domineering, conceited
Mr. Goon. 'One of them is, I believe, that clever
boy—the one who has helped us in so many mysteries
—Frederick Trotteville ! '

Goon opened and shut his mouth like a goldfish and for two minutes couldn't say a single word. He went slowly purple and the Inspector looked at him in alarm.

'You'll have a heart-attack one of these days, Goon, if you get so angry,' he said. 'Surely you don't mind Frederick coming over? You are quite sure you have solved the case yourself, and arrested the right people—so what is there to worry about?'

'I'm not worrying,' said Goon, fiercely. 'That boy—that toad—begging your pardon, sir—always interfering with the Law—always . . .'

'Now Goon, he *helps* the Law, he doesn't interfere with it,' said the Inspector.

Goon muttered something about toads and turnip-heads, and then subsided into deep gloom. Pippin coming—and all those dratted children. What was UP?

Pippin duly arrived with Alec Grant, the five children, and, of course, Buster. Goon's face grew even blacker when he saw Buster, who greeted him with frantic joy, as if he was an old friend, tearing round his feet in a most exasperating way.

'Ah, Frederick—so you're on the job again,' said the Inspector. 'Pleased to see you. Hallo, Larry—Pip—Daisy—and here's little Bets too. Have they turned you out of the Find-Outers yet, Bets?'

'Turned her out! I should think not,' said Fatty. 'If it hadn't been for Bets we'd never have hit on the right solution.'

There was a growl from Goon at this. The Inspector turned to him. 'Ah, Goon—you also think you have hit on the right solution, don't you?' he said. 'Your two arrests are in the other room.

Now—what makes you think you have solved the case correctly, Goon ? You were just about to tell me when I got Pippin's telephone call.'

' Sir, there's a confession here from Boysie Summers, the Pantomime Cat,' said Goon. ' Says as clear as a pike-staff that he did the job, with Zoe Markham to help him. This here's her handker-chief, found on the verandah on the night of the crime—Z, for Zoe, in the corner, sir.'

' Oh ! ' said Daisy. ' That's *my* old hanky, Inspector ! And I put the Z in the corner, just for a joke. Didn't I, you others ? '

The other four nodded at once. ' It's certainly not Zoe's,' said Daisy. ' She'd never have a dirty, torn old hanky like this. I should have thought Mr. Goon would have guessed that.'

Mr. Goon began to breathe heavily. ' Now look here ! ' he began.

' Wait, Goon,' said the Inspector, picking up the ' confession.' ' So this is what Boysie said, is it ? Bring him in, please, Pippin. He and Zoe are in the next room. They can both come in.'

Pippin went to fetch Zoe and Boysie. Zoe was in tears, and so upset that she didn't even seem to see the five children. She went straight up to the Inspector and tapped the ' confession ' he held in his hand.

' Not one word of that is true ! ' she said. ' Not one word ! *He* forced Boysie to say things that weren't true. Look at Boysie—can you imagine him doing a crime like that, even with my help ? He's nothing but a child, for all he's twenty-four. That policeman badgered him and terrified him and threatened him till poor Boysie was so frightened he said anything. Anything! It's wicked, really *wicked*!'

Boysie stood beside her. The children hardly knew him, out of his cat-skin. He did seem only a child—a child that trembled and shook and clutched at Zoe's dress. Bets felt the tears coming into her eyes.

'Well, Miss Markham,' said Inspector Jenks, 'we have here some one else for questioning. I think you know him.'

Zoe turned and saw Alec. 'Alec Grant!' she said. 'Did *you* do it, Alec? Alec, if you did, say so. Would you let poor Boysie be sent *right* off his head with this, if you could help it? You hated the manager. You always said so. Did *you* do it?'

Alec said nothing. The Inspector turned to Pippin. 'Pippin—will you say why you have brought this man here, please?'

Pippin began his tale. He told it extremely well and lucidly. It was plain to see that P.C. Pippin would one day make a very good policeman indeed!

The Inspector interrupted occasionally to ask a question, and sometimes Fatty had to put a few words in too. Goon sat with his mouth open, his eyes almost bulging out of his head.

Alec Grant looked more and more uncomfortable as time went on. When Pippin and Fatty between them related how the children had gone to Sheepridge and seen the different autograph in Julia's album—which Pippin placed before the Inspector as evidence—he turned very pale.

'So you think this man here got his twin-sister to impersonate him, whilst he slipped back to the theatre, doped Boysie, got into the cat-skin, took up a doped cup of tea to the manager, robbed the safe, and then pulled the skin on the sleeping Boysie again ? ' said Inspector Jenks. ' A most ingenious crime. We must get on to this man's twin-sister. We must pull her in too.'

' Here ! ' said Goon, in a strangled sort of voice. ' I can't have this. I tell you that man's not the culprit—he *didn't* do it. Haven't I got that confession there for you to see ? '

And then poor Goon got a terrible shock. ' I *did* do it ! ' said Alec Grant. ' Exactly as P.C. Pippin described it. But leave my sister out of it, *please* ! She knows nothing about it at all ! I telephoned her and begged her to take my place at the concert, and she did. She's done that before when I've felt ill, and nobody has known. We're as alike as peas. I impersonate women, as you know—and who's to know the difference if my sister impersonates *me* ? No one ! Only these kids—they're too clever by half ! '

Inspector Jenks took the ' confession ' and tore it in half. ' There's a fire behind you, Goon,' he said, in a cold voice. ' Put this in, will you ? '

And Goon had to put the wonderful ' confession ' into the fire and watch it burn. He wished he could sink through the floor. He wished he was at the other end of the world. If ever cruelty and stupidity and conceit were punished well and truly, then they were punished now, in the person of Goon.

' I've got all the money,' said Alec. ' I meant to give it back, really. It was just to give the manager a nasty shock—he's a mean old beast. If I'd known Boysie and Zoe were arrested I'd have owned up.'

' You *did* know,' said Pippin, quietly. ' No good saying that now.'

'Well,' said the Inspector, leaning back and looking at the children. 'Well! Once more you appear to have come to our rescue, children. I'm much obliged to you, Pippin, my congratulations—you handled this case well, in spite of being forbidden to work with Goon. Frederick, you are incorrigible and irrepressible—and if you place any more false clues I shall probably be forced to arrest you! You are also a very great help, and most ingenious in your tackling of any problem. Thanks very much!'

The Inspector beamed round at the five children and Pippin, including Zoe and Boysie in his smile. Bets slipped her hand into his. 'You don't *really* mean you'd arrest Fatty?' she said, anxiously. 'We were all as bad as he was with those clues and things, Inspector.'

'No. I was pulling his leg,' said the Inspector. 'Not that I approve of that sort of behaviour at all, you understand—very reprehensible indeed— but I can't help feeling that what you all did later has quite cancelled out what came before! And now, do you know what time it is? Two o'clock. Has any one had any lunch?'

Nobody had, and the children suddenly became aware of a very hollow feeling in their middles.

'Well, I hope you will do me the honour of lunching with me at the Royal Hotel,' said the Inspector. 'I'll get some one to telephone your families, who will no doubt be searching the countryside for you now! And perhaps Miss Zoe would come too—and er—the Pantomime Cat?'

'Oh, thank you,' said Zoe, all smiles. 'Are we quite free now?'

'Quite,' said the Inspector. 'Goon, take this fellow Grant away. And wait here till I come back. I shall have a few words to say to you.'

Goon, looking like a pricked balloon, took Alec Grant away. Bets heaved a sigh of relief. 'Oh, Inspector Jenks, I was *so* afraid you'd ask Mr. Goon to come out to lunch too!'

'Not on your life!' said the Inspector. 'Oh, you're there too, Pippin. Go and get yourself a good meal in the police-station canteen, and then come back here and write out a full report of this case for me. And ring the children's parents, will you?'

Pippin saluted and grinned. He was very bucked with himself. He winked at Fatty and Fatty winked back. Aha! There would be a spot of promotion for Pippin if he went on handling cases like this.

'I've really enjoyed this mystery,' said Bets, as she sat down at a hotel table and unfolded a snowy-white napkin. 'It was very, very difficult—but it wasn't frightening at all.'

'Oh yes it was—to me and Boysie,' said Zoe. She filled a glass with lemonade and held it up to the children.

'Here's to you!' she cried. 'The Five Find-Outers—and Dog!'

The Inspector raised his glass too, and grinned. 'Here's to the great detectives—who solved the insoluble and most mysterious case in their career —the Mystery of the Pantomime Cat!'

PRINTED BY
MORRISON AND GIBB LTD.,
LONDON AND EDINBURGH